A BORDER STATION

D1102298

www.penguin.co.uk

Also by Shane Connaughton

A
BORDER
STATION

—

SHANE
CONNAUGHTON

BLACK SWAN IRELAND

TRANSWORLD PUBLISHERS
61–63 Uxbridge Road, London W5 5SA
www.penguin.co.uk

Transworld is part of the Penguin Random House group of companies
whose addresses can be found at global.penguinrandomhouse.com

Penguin
Random House
UK

First published in Great Britain in 1989 by Hamish Hamilton Ltd
A Penguin Random House company
Black Swan Ireland edition published 2017

'Topping' and the Hennessy Literary Award winner
'Beatrice' were first published in the *Irish Press*

A CIP catalogue record for this book
is available from the British Library.

ISBN 9781784162559

Typeset in 11/14.25 pt Sabon LT Std by Jouve (UK), Milton Keynes
Printed and bound in Great Britain by Clays Ltd, Bungay, Suffolk

Penguin Random House is committed to a sustainable
future for our business, our readers and our planet. This book
is made from Forest Stewardship Council® certified paper.

1 3 5 7 9 10 8 6 4 2

FOR ANN

CONTENTS

TOPPING

T HE ROAD WAS DRY, dusty and pockmarked with potholes. You had to keep swerving to avoid them. When you didn't you could feel the jagged edges dunting the rim of the front wheel.

'Keep into the side,' his father shouted back at him.

It was easier along the side but his bicycle gathered speed there and that was dangerous. The brakes weren't good. In fact he only had half a one. A worn-down block of rubber which did little more than clean one side of the back wheel. Crashing into his father was a nightmare to be avoided at all costs.

The bell didn't work. And the saddle was no good either. It kept tipping forward and he had to reach between his legs to adjust it back into position. He stayed in the middle of the road and let the potholes serve as brakes. 'Sure isn't that what they're for?' he heard one of the Guards joke to his father. 'Have you ever met a Cavan man yet with brakes on his bicycle?'

It was a lost part of the world, this. No tarred roads,

no running water in the houses, no electric light and outside lavatories full of brown and wet and newspaper. The clinging smell of Elsan and when the lavatory was full burying the contents down the bottom of the garden.

He knew his mother wasn't happy here.

His father rode on in front, pressing with measured energy on the pedals, letting the exercise do him good.

Earlier he had watched him eating his dinner in the same mechanical way. His jaws pedalling up and down on the roast chicken, potatoes, carrots, cabbage and two helpings of rhubarb pie. Grinding out the goodness. A short nap and then this trip out to see the football match was just what the digestive system needed. Routine and a well-regulated stomach were the keys to long life. And eventually Heaven. His father had read as much in the *Garda Review*.

As they rode along, hedges, hills, dandelions and swampy fields skirted the way. Cattle, standing in the half-dried mud of gateways, stared at them. A pair of cackling magpies flitted across the road and landed on a rusty barrel lying abandoned in the middle of the field.

'Well, there's two of them in it anyway,' his father said. One for sorrow, two for joy . . .

His father had two big fists. They gripped the handlebars raw and red. Even in warm weather they looked cold. The knuckles crinkled with tight skin, like a chicken's leg. The rubber grips on the handlebar ends were lost in the coil of his fingers.

His feet were big too. He wore boots, the long laces

double-wrapped round the uppers and tied in a knotted bow just below the second hole from the top. 'Always give the ankle a bit of leeway.'

His trouser ends were folded neat and clipped up on the calf so the knee action wouldn't round out the regulation-sharp seams.

His dark-blue uniform moved through the country-side like a cloud. The truncheon in its black leather sheath belted to the tunic. The truncheon had grooves round the top and a loop of brown leather through which you put your hand so it couldn't be snatched away. His father had shown him how to grip it.

The truncheon was heavy and shone like chestnut.

They came out from the hills and into a flat stretch. To the right towards the Six Counties the land was even, green and healthy-looking. To the left, though, there was only mile after mile of rushy fields, marsh, lakes and bog. 'By cripes,' muttered his father, 'they knew what they were doing when they drew that Border.'

Suddenly he slowed down. There was something ahead. The boy, drawing level with him, deliberately steered into a pothole rather than pass him out.

They were going so slowly now the spokes no longer blurred.

In the distance, on a piece of grass between the road and the hedge, something was hanging. It looked like a brown sheet.

'Fecking tinkers,' said his father, 'and just inside my sub-district.'

They drew nearer the encampment. The brown sheet

was a piece of canvas flung across hoops of some kind to form a tent.

A turf fire smouldered at its entrance. A green and yellow painted spring-cart was upended at the back of the tent, the graceful shafts curving to the sky. A horse was tethered to the wheel.

A young stout woman squatted in front of the fire, poking life into it with a cabbage stalk.

His father got off his bike and stood looking at her. She refused to look up. Flames spurted.

The horse moved its rump against the cart, shifting its weight from a hind leg. The boy looked at the woman but looked quickly away in case she caught his eye.

As his father continued staring at her, her face became sullen. But she wouldn't look up and recognise his existence. She had seen them approaching. The uniform. The peaked cap. The silver buttons. She knew well they were there. Arresting her peace with hostile eyes.

His father nodded a few times, whistling quietly as he did so, then remounted his bicycle and pedalled on.

The boy surprised by the move was left stranded for a few seconds. The tinker woman looked up at him. Her brown eyes books of knowledge beyond his power.

A man's face peeped from the slit entrance to the tent.

The boy jumped on his bike and rode quickly along the verge.

Why had his father left the tinkers alone?

Down a laneway they saw a whitewashed house with a window box of red flowers. The nearby sheds were whitewashed too. It had to be a Protestant house. Cleanliness was part of their religion.

Onto the hills on the left, through a gap in the hedge, tore a pack of beagles. Strung out in line they snaked across the fields trumpeting their mad hunger into the air. Behind them pounded shouting men in wellington boots and carrying sticks.

'God help the poor hare if them savages catch him. The two-legged ones!' Like a belch, the jibe came from deep within his father: the words flung with a sharp sideways flick of the head at the backs of the ragged mob of hunters. They watched the last of them disappear behind a clump of withered trees. The boy knew expressing contempt was exercise. His father got rid of bile that way. He looked down at the road flying beneath his wheels. It sped out between his legs like a river in spate.

There was a thick black line on his white sock. Oil. The chain wasn't cased. His mother would scold him. But her words wouldn't hurt.

In bed with his mother was the warmest place in the world. Hay. Honey.

'Out the hell outa the way! Ye mangy beggars!' roared his father. Goats tethered in pairs wandered in the middle of the road. Like wet blackcurrants, faeces spilled from under their tails. Cupfuls of them. The thick smell from their coarse-haired bodies could almost be tasted.

'Their stink has me stunk, Daddy.'

'And they call this the country of little hills and lakes,'

shouted his father, as they steered through the scattering herd, 'the county of goats and potholes is the right title.'

Soon they left the pockmarked road behind and with a final rattle bumped up onto the tarred main road linking Cavan, Clones and the North. Turning right they headed towards the Border and the football field. He pedalled up to his father's shoulder. His father with a grin on the side of his mouth glanced at him.

A contest.

They stopped pedalling and free-wheeled.

Which bike would be the last to wobble to a halt?

His father's was heavier, had bigger wheels and was well looked-after. He oiled it regularly and wiped it down with a cloth especially if it had been out in the rain. The rims shone, the wheels ran true, the spokes were tight, the cranks glistened, the reflector gleamed and the bell was bright as the belt buckle on his uniform. 'Tin Lizzie', he called it.

'I've looked after her. So she looks after me.'

'How old is she, Daddy?'

'She was old when I bought her. And that's thirty years ago. That'll give you some idea. A Rudge. You couldn't beat her with a drumstick.'

They free-wheeled along, his father gaining momentum, the boy beginning to drop behind.

He didn't mind losing. In fact he had to. Because if his father lost at anything he would bring a mood down on the world thick as tar.

In the silent Border countryside above the gentle

ticking of turning wheels they could hear the distant baying of the pack of beagles.

He looked again at the oil mark on his sock.

White ankle-socks. The tinker woman wore ankle-socks too. Green ones. Her legs were brown with dirt and weather. She belonged to the man in the tent. A slit of white eyes, alert and dangerous. Green ankle-socks.

The mudguards rattled as he wobbled to a halt.

'I've lost, Daddy.'

'Ah-hah, ya boya,' his father shouted back in triumph. He was pleased.

'If we can't fight a war, any little victory will do. That's what your grandfather used to say RIP.'

They reached the Border. A slight difference in level and texture of the tarmacadam was all that indicated they were passing into what was supposed to be a foreign country. But further along they came to a row of iron spikes stuck across the road. It was a measure aimed at the IRA. But the locals had bulldozed between the hedge and the nearest spike, making a deep-rutted muddy path wide enough for the use of cars, lorries and tractors. His father dismounted and looked at the spikes. Then he reached out and with his hands tested their strength. The boy did the same.

Rusty flakes on the brown girders. Railway lines sticking up from Hell. For the next mile the Border zig-zagged crazily so that one minute his father would announce they were in the North, the next minute the South.

'Whilst grass is green and water runs, as long as that

7

Border is there, this country will never be at peace,'
declaimed his father and went on to repeat it a number
of times. As if repetition would turn the words into a
political fact so blatant even a fool could see it.

Peace. Why weren't his mother and father at peace?
Why did he thump his mother's bedroom door at night,
trying to get in to her? What kind of peace was that?
And why when they sat to eat was his hand under
the table on her knee, her ankle trapped in the twist
of his great black boots? Once when his spoon fell on
the floor and he went under the table to retrieve it, he
saw her hand trying to push his hand away from her
flesh. Why?

They rode on but his bicycle bell fell off and went
hopping into the ditch. They searched but couldn't find
it, his father lashing at the long grass and nettles,
tramping them down with brute force. The boy knew
his father was angry. He valued things like bent nails,
odd buttons, buckets without handles, sewing needles
with the eyes snapped off . . . bicycle bells.

'There it is, Daddy!'

His father bent to pick it up but it was only a stone.

'Ah, get away out of that, you nigget.'

He flung the stone into the ditch and looked at the
countryside and the sky above it.

'What on God's earth did I do to deserve being sent
here to this cursed hole? Civilisation as far away as the
dark side of the stars!'

'Mammy's not happy here either.'

'How do you know?'

'Ah . . . she . . . she told me.'

His father glared at him, his eyes bright as the badge on his cap.

'Did she indeed?'

'And I'm not happy as well.'

'Why not?'

How could you tell anyone why you were unhappy? Especially your father!

'Because . . . because this bloody bike is breaking my heart.'

'This WHAT bike?'

'This . . . RUSTY bike.'

'Don't get too big for your boots, me buck. I heard what you said. There's nothing wrong with that bike. It's the way you ride it.'

'But it's falling to bits, Daddy.'

'It's a poor jockey blames his horse. When I was your age I had to WALK everywhere.'

'I'd prefer to walk.'

'Get on that bike! Move!'

Tears came into his eyes and, though he knew it was dangerous, he heard himself shouting at his father.

'I want to go home to Mammy!'

He expected a crack from his father's fist but instead his father looked steadily at him and said, as if challenging him, 'So do I. So do I!'

Why should he want to go home? He turned away from his father's eyes and stared into the ditch. Right at the bottom, water seeped through the weeds and a dandelion clock took off and floated above their heads.

Getting on the bikes they rode towards the football pitch. When they got there, the rival supporters were gathered on opposite sides of the field. The teams were out, the visitors in red, Butlershill in blue and yellow hoops.

Though people spoke to his father they stood away from him. Beside the uniform they felt they couldn't swear at the players with customary abandon.

His father stood in front of his bike, his rump resting on the crossbar. Everyone else slung their bikes in tangled heaps on the ground. The match started and almost immediately a fight broke out. Punches and kicks were swapped and soon spectators had joined in, some of them rolling about in the mud in their Sunday suits seemingly trying to strangle one another.

The boy looked down at the streak of oil on his sock.

'Arrest them, Sergeant,' a man shouted.

'Arrest the bloody referee,' shouted a woman, 'he's the one started it.'

But his father grinned at them, took off his cap, breathed over the silver badge, wiped it with his sleeve and returning the cap to his head said, 'When they get fed up they'll stop of their own accord.'

They did.

Up the other end of the field away from the game the boy saw a hare carefully hopping along, stopping every few yards, ears cocked, checking the distant clamour of the crowd. Some other boys had noticed it too and gave chase. The hare sprung above the long grass and with swift lanky bounds made for a gap in the far hedge.

'Come on,' said his father, 'this standard of football is too bad to be true.'

They rode homewards, a brooding look on his father's face.

Nearing the spikes across the road, they saw an Army jeep blocking the bulldozed pathway.

Soldiers looked out at them, rifles resting between their knees.

'Cripes,' said his father, 'it's the British.'

Standing by the jeep was an officer. He was tall, handsome, blond-haired and round his neck wore a red cravat. Drawing level with him the officer saluted his father, who saluted back.

'Grand day now,' said his father.

'Topping,' replied the officer. A soldier winked at the boy.

'Everything all right your side, Sergeant?'

'Yes. Thank God. Why wouldn't they be?'

They didn't await a reply but rode swiftly out of Fermanagh, his father pleased at his religious and political swipe at the Forces of the Queen.

When they came onto the potholed road the boy dropped behind. He had noticed his father was looking grim, muttering, churning himself into a temper. He would now look for an excuse to explode it.

Before they even got to them he knew they were going to stop at the tinker's encampment.

His father was pedalling with purpose, making for

somewhere definite. And it wasn't home. Tea wouldn't be ready for another hour at least. It had to be the tinkers. What was he going to do to them?

When the upturned cart was in sight his father slowed down, pulling on the brakes with a jerk of his shoulders. When a little nearer he swung his right leg to the same side as his left and, standing on one pedal, scootered to an eventual stop.

The fire this time was well banked round with turf and on the busy flames rested a black pan of sausages and rashers. The tinker woman squatted by the fire, her hand on the pan handle.

'Smells good,' said his father, surprising her with his easy tone, so that she looked up at him. 'Where's your man?'

'He's not here,' replied the woman. The boy looked at her green ankle-socks. His father rested his bicycle against the cart and was about to look into the tent when the man came out.

'He's here now,' said his father, with laconic sarcasm.

The tinker wore brown boots, a faded brown suit, an open-necked shirt and a hat.

His face was tight, compact, chiselled, attractive, shifty. His skin was very white and on his upper lip was a pencil-thin moustache.

His dancing eyes flickered from the uniform to the frying pan. The smoke curving up the side of the pan went straight into the still air. Silence was a tactic of his father's, during which he sized up his quarry. The woman stared into the pan; the man shifted from foot to foot.

'What ails you?' queried the tinker.

'Where did you get that turf?'

The tinker swung towards the fire. The flames spurted. So that was it. Stolen turf. What harm was it, thought the boy to himself, even if it was stolen?

'Sure the bog's full of it,' said the woman, echoing his thoughts.

On the other side of the hedge was a brown stretch of water, reedy, treacherous-looking bogland.

The banks were too poor and unformed for turf to be harvested in the normal way. Mud was shovelled out from wet holes, spread on the banks, cut into rough shapes with the back of the hand and left to dry. The sods were much bigger and not as neat as cut turf but the local people claimed there was 'ojus burning' in them.

His father stepped towards the tinker.

The horse turned its head and stared at the uniform.

'The farmer gave me it,' said the tinker, gesturing towards the whitewashed house in the distance.

'Did he now? We'll go and ask him.'

The tinker looked at the woman. She took the pan from the flames.

The boy was left alone with her.

She put the pan on the ground. The sizzling faded. Squatting down she pressed her dress between her legs and stared at the boy with cold fury, trying to hurt him because of his father.

He tried to look away but her eyes held him tight. She bounced up and down on her hunkers, her thumb in her mouth. Staring at him. Her eyes big as moons. He clung to his bicycle unable to move out of her gaze. Panic gripped him. He tried to lick his lips but his tongue was dry. He was conscious of his eyes blinking and then to his amazement he felt his grip loosen and saw his bike clatter to the road, one of the handlebars resting in a pothole puddle.

In a trance he hauled the bike up and tried to stare at the front wheel but his eyes were pulled towards the woman's.

'Do you eat sweets?'

'I do,' he whispered.

'Pity I haven't got any,' and she rocked over and back with laughter. He felt ashamed and angry. If his father didn't return soon he was going to jump on the bike and cycle like mad for home.

The woman's attention was diverted to the horse, which had pulled at its tether and begun to urinate.

It gushed out from under its tail onto the grass verge and flooded into the road, foam swirling on top.

'Good girl, Dolly,' said the woman.

A she. Like her. Like his mother. Not like him.

Getting up she went to the back of the tent and came back with a bucket, soap and a creamery can. She poured water from the can into the bucket. Kicking off her shoes she lifted a foot onto the rim of the creamery can and began to peel away her ankle-sock with the hook of her thumb. When half off she scratched her heel before rolling the sock away completely. Admiring her neat foot she wiggled her toes and searched between them with her fingers. Unlike her legs her feet were white and clean.

As she took off her other sock, her dress fell back along her thigh so that the boy saw the far flesh and curved moon of her rump.

White like her feet. Like flour.

He looked at the horse and back to the woman.

She began to wash her socks. Green soapy suds in her mashing fingers. Flies buzzing round the dying foam on the roadway.

'What the hell are you looking at?'

Not knowing where they came from or why, the boy heard the words 'Not much' coming out of his mouth. The woman's eyes narrowed, but then she smiled at him.

'Well, aren't you the spoilt wee pup?'

His father often said that to him. Spoilt. But he only said it when his mother was listening. It was like a secret word, the use of which they knew would start a row.

When his mother hugged him she was warm through her clothes, her apron, even through an overcoat. His father's uniform was cold and smelt of ink.

The tinker woman looked warm. As a cake coming out of the oven. She continued washing the socks, ignoring him for some time as she rinsed, squeezed and then hung them on a bush.

They were a lighter green than the velvet green in a magpie's tail. Lighter than ivy. Than moss. Grass green.

She squatted back down on her hunkers by the fire.

He found he wasn't afraid of her now. Her face, her hair, her dress, her white feet were pleasant to look at.

'Where are you from?' he asked shyly, but with a growing feeling of superiority. She laughed, her teeth flashing in her open mouth.

'Give us a kiss and I'll tell you. Just a little one, like you give your mammy.'

The last two words she rolled round her mouth, curdling them, before spitting them out with a venom that cut straight into him.

A surge of panic gripped him again and once more he was on the point of jumping on his bike and making for home. But he was powerless to move. Besides, what would his father say if he disappeared just like that?

He noticed his fists gripping the handlebars, knuckles glistening with tension.

He felt dizzy and believed he was at any moment going to faint.

The woman stood up.

'Give that to me!' she commanded.

He had no idea what she meant. Now she was pointing at him.

With dread at the consequences, when his father found out, he feared she was going to take his bicycle. That's what tinkers did! They even committed murder!!

His legs were weakening and but for the bike propping him up he would have clattered down into a heap on the roadside.

'It's streaky black,' he heard her saying, but didn't understand, 'I'll wash it for you.'

She stood looking at him, waiting for him to obey her, impatient at his stupidity.

'Your sock,' she shouted, 'I'll wash it for you.'

'Wash it? It?' The words burbled silently round his head. Then they hit him. Now he realised. She wanted to wash his oil-streaked sock.

Never. Never. His mother wouldn't be pleased. A tinker woman wash his sock? He'd be a laughing stock. Oh no. Never. He couldn't.

But, as if outside his body, he watched himself laying down his bike, going on one knee, untying his shoe, taking off his ankle-sock and handing it to her. If his father came back now and saw him standing with one foot bare, and the wife of the tinker he was about to arrest washing his sock, there'd be ructions when he got home.

He looked up the road towards the whitewashed house. They were coming back. And there was his sock in the bucket of suds. He'd never get it back in time. His stomach churned and he noticed he was dancing from one foot to the other. She had the oily part of the sock in a washingboard grip of knuckles and fingers and was rubbing another part of the sock against it, trying to get rid of the stain.

He could only think of how wet the sock looked and how it would be impossible to dry it, iron it and get it back on before his father reached them.

The woman looked at him and followed his gaze. But she didn't hurry when she saw the men approaching. With a soapy hand she flicked the hair from the side of her face revealing a big ear-ring, smiled at the boy and carried on washing. His father and the tinker were now only about fifty yards away.

He slipped his foot into his shoe and tried to hide his naked ankle by holding it close to his other leg.

The woman flung the suddy water over the hedge, poured fresh water and began to rinse the sock just as the men reached them.

His father looked grim. Now the woman had the sock by the toe and was whirling it through the clear water. Almost playing with it.

Surely his father must have noticed.

'I'm taking your man into the barracks with me,' he said to the woman. Maybe he hadn't.

'But his tea's ready,' said the woman with limp defiance.

'He'll be back,' said his father, 'when I'm done with him.' He went to her, took the bucket of water from her and dowsed the fire with a sizzling splash.

The woman was furious. She tore at his face with her eyes, the boy's ankle-sock dangling from her fingers.

Her man went into the tent. His father took four half-burnt sods from the quenched fire, put two on the carrier of his bike and handed two to the boy.

'You bring these,' he ordered. 'And don't lose them – they're evidence.'

The tinker came rushing out of the tent, and going to the horse, untied it and leaped on its back.

The sleepy animal taken by surprise staggered about in the middle of the road not knowing what was going on. A quick crack on its neck with the halter and a couple of heels in the belly brought it to the required reality and, in a cloud of dust it galloped away, the tinker clutching down his hat with one hand.

His father swung his leg over his bike, his great boot momentarily hanging in the air as he adjusted himself on the saddle; then ramming down hard on the pedal, head down, back crouched, he rode after the tinker.

The tinker rode flat out only to be awkward. Not to escape. He knew he couldn't.

Once again the boy was alone with the woman.

She stood for a moment looking after the boy's father, then at the dowsed fire, than at the boy. Lifting up her dress to reveal her knees she sunk to the ground.

'God blast his face with warts and wrinkles and that he may die roarin'. And that's my solemn curse this day,' she roared to the sky.

The boy knew why she had bared her knees. His mother told him once that with love or curses you had to have flesh. Now he knew what she meant. Partly anyway.

'My sock, please,' he said to the woman.

Her eyes narrowed, and breathing heavily after the effort of cursing she seemed about to attack him but then with a weary sigh she sunk to her hunkers and just looked at him, almost in an appealing way.

She still held on to his sock.

He was worried. He didn't want to be left too far behind. He wanted to show his father how capable he was by bringing his share of the evidence swiftly and safely to the Station.

But he couldn't arrive without his ankle-sock. He would have to, somehow, get it back from her.

'How would you like to join the tinkers?' the woman asked, her teeth smiling, shining.

His heart thumped up inside him. He sloped his bicycle at an angle the better to get his leg quickly across the bar. He would have to go home without the sock and think of some lie to tell on the way. And later in bed with his mother tell the truth.

'Where the hell do you think you're going?' shouted the woman.

The boy was sure she was going to capture him. Murder him. Kiss him. And keep him forever.

He moved off but the front wheel went into a pothole, stopping him dead. He struggled for balance but the bike lurched over and he had to scramble off, the jolt knocking the two sods of turf on to the road.

Holding the bike with one hand he bent to pick them up with the other. One of the sods crumbled to pieces. He began to cry. Little anguished whimpers of fear and anger.

He stuffed some of the pieces into his pockets and managed to secure the other sod on his carrier.

As he mounted the bike again he couldn't resist looking at the woman.

A breeze was sifting through her hair and tucking her dress about her body. She coiled his sock into the ball of her fist and flung it at him. It hit him right between the eyes and fell down on to his crossbar and then to the road.

Her face was fierce and proud and sad.

The green ankle-socks flapped drying on the hedge.

'Come back, nice boy. Come back, angel.'

He managed to get moving, his legs growing stronger the further he got from her. But even a long way away he thought he could hear her hysterical laughter following him along the wind.

When he got near the Station he saw the tinker's horse tied to the barracks gate. It had assumed its lazy-leg posture of the encampment.

He went into the day room with his 'evidence'. His sense of achievement diminished by the loss of his sock.

But neither his father nor the tinker was there.

He put the turf on the table. Then he heard muffled groans and raised voices. Startled, he went into the hallway to listen. Silence. Frightened, he tiptoed along the tiled corridor and, though he had decided to get out of the barracks, instinctively he stopped at the cell door. He knew they were in there. Behind the massive door, all bolts, locks and hinges.

A big bunch of keys dangled from a keyhole. Rooted to the spot he listened in the terrifying silence. Why weren't they making a noise now? His neck was craned at an unnatural angle, the tension hurting.

A strangulated cry of temper tore through the thick wooden door. That was his father.

'You broke into that lock-up shop, didn't you? Come on, admit it. And you can go.'

The boy ran outside. The horse looked up, pointing its ears forward.

His father was beating the tinker. It wasn't fair. He'd missed his tea and now he was being beaten! And his woman was nice.

The Station was a large yellow-coloured pebble-dashed bungalow with separate entrances to the married quarters and barracks. The outhouses were separate too and the vegetable gardens divided by a high wall.

His father didn't allow him at the back of the police quarters, but he raced round, got a ladder from an outhouse and put it up against the outer wall of the cell.

The tinker was screaming.

A slit in the wall let daylight into the cell. Peering in he could see his father's cap and another head with a bald spot on it. That was Guard McMurray.

'You broke in there and anything you couldn't take you stood on! Butter, cameras, bread, radios, eggs ... didn't you?' shouted his father.

For a split second he saw the tinker's face. Blood came from his nose. This wasn't fair. It just wasn't. He wanted to shout 'Stop', but he couldn't. He heard himself shout 'Hello', instead. He felt foolish.

The bodies in the slit of light stopped swirling and he saw his father flash a look up at him.

'It's going to rain, Daddy,' he said, surprised at his calmness and the stupidity of the remark.

There were murmurs from Guard McMurray and he heard the cell door banging open.

Getting down from the ladder he ran to the front of the building. To keep a distance between himself and his father he went out the gate and sat on the opposite side of the road.

Minutes later the tinker came out. He had his hat in his hand. He untied his horse, got on it, but not as nimbly as before and throwing a sideways glance at the boy galloped away.

His father came out and walked towards the married quarters. The boy called out to him.

'I left the evidence on the table, Daddy.'

His father stared over at him.

'Come here, you.'

The boy was afraid but he knew he had to go.

His father took him gently by the hand and they walked in together. His mother had the tea ready. The boy sat in to the table, keeping his naked ankle well under. So far no one had noticed.

His father chewed his food methodically. Masticating, he called it.

His mother played with crumbs in silence. Staring down at the willow-patterned plate.

The silence was broken by his father grumbling out from deep within his thoughts.

' "Topping", he said to me, the beggar. "Topping".'

The boy laughed. His father looked at him.

'You tell your mammy what happened to your ankle-sock. You spoilt wee pup you.'

His mother glanced up, her moon eyes flashing fire.

Squirming away from them, he slid to the floor.

Under the table his mother's ankle was entwined in his father's boots and his hand gripped her knee, the dress pushed up along her thigh. He sat back up at the table.

On the mantelpiece was a picture of God. His eyes watched them and the clock ticked the silence away.

BEATRICE

THE DEMESNE WALL, CRUMBLING under an age of
ivy, snaked for miles round a vast estate of land,
orchards, trees and lakes.

The wall was a green snake with an endless belly.
Where the stonework bulged to bursting that was the
serpent's undigested food.

In the heart of the demesne lived Lady Sarah
Butler-Coote, an octogenarian spinster and the last of
her line.

They were on the way to see her.

His father had shaved before coming out and stood in
front of the mirror brushing the grey out of his hair with
boot polish.

'Darling I am growing old, silver threads amongst the
gold . . .' sang his mother, and his father flashed her a
sharp look from the corner of the glass. He smiled.

'I'll knock on your door tonight, hah?' On the hill
behind the barracks a dog barked.

'Not till that animal shites leather.'

'In that case,' replied his father, 'I'll leave out an old boot for its supper.' His mother laughed.

Preening and whistling, his father admired himself then, bunching his uniform buttons in a brass button-stick, began shining them with a Brasso-stained rag.

'What are you looking at? Go and get the bikes ready.'

Outside he heard the struggling and his mother protesting – 'Later, later.'

As they rode through the main gates to the desmesne he wondered what it was his father wanted from her. Why was there always such stern mystery in his face?

The massive gates were hung on stone pillars, each with a sculpted acorn on top.

From the gatehouse a man waved to them. He stood in the open door, a birdcage hanging above his head. He had a few days' growth of beard, his belly bulged from his dirty shirt and his simpleton grin as he waved frightened the boy.

'Poor Mickey. Less brains than a bucket. And isn't he the happy man?'

'How, Daddy, if he's no brains?'

'Watch where you're steering or you'll wreck that bike entirely!'

They were on the way to ask Lady Sarah for some firewood. Trees tossed by the wind or trees in danger of falling were sold off to the people. Bits of wood no bigger than a man's arm were given free. His father called this ancient right estovers. His father knew the law inside out and backwards. He sometimes practised on him.

'What's pannage?'

'The right to let your pigs root in the forest for nuts, yes?'

'Good boy.'

'But we haven't got pigs, Daddy.'

'What's that got to do with the price of onions?'

He liked the woods with its deep pools of damp light lying beneath the trees but he didn't like riding his bicycle along the drive leading to Coote House. Certain stretches, in an attempt to render the endless potholes harmless, were strewn with rough gravel inches thick so that riding over it was as great a struggle as trying to run through deep water.

Mudguards rattling, the bike juddered and jarred him from the saddle. For relief he steered on to the grassy verge but, the soft ground giving way, he skidded down into a clump of rhododendrons. Tangled in a sea of greenery a bloom and blush of flowers danced wildly above his head. Spiders ran pell-mell along his legs. A frog peeped at him from a bed of wet leaves.

'I won't touch you if you don't touch me.'

The frog leaped towards him, its slimy body landing on his ankle. With a startled shriek he struggled from the bushes and hauled his bike back on to the drive.

The seat of his pants was damp from the wet earth. Clammy on his skin it reminded him of the frog.

His father, ploughing on ahead, had reached the smooth part of the drive round by the lake. He was looking back, waiting.

He grabbed the handlebars and instead of mounting ran alongside his bike until he too reached the smooth.

His father's eyes could bend bottles.

'What the hell are you playing at?'

'This is my horse and I'm a Red Indian.'

He felt foolish always having to follow his father everywhere. Like a foal after a stallion.

His father sat on his motionless bicycle, one foot on a pedal, the other on the ground. He searched the boy's pale face as if looking for a clue. His eyes made you feel like a criminal. They were gripping bright like the silver sugar-tongs his mother kept in the parlour.

Then he noticed his father wasn't looking at him at all. His eyes had glazed over, like the sugar-tongs when you breathed on them.

A silence could last an hour. Sometimes when his mother was involved it could last all day. And the next day as well.

In a silence his father's face was a pile of stones. 'You're some Cherokee all right,' he muttered at last and they rode onwards.

The drive was lined with ancient trees. Great oaks, massive chestnut, raggedy elm and magnificent copper beeches.

Out on the lake the silver evening lay still as a stopped clock.

His father shouted back to him. 'You're a good boy, Dan.'

'And you're a good daddy, Daddy.'

His father's shoulders still shook with laughter as they turned into the straight leading up to Coote House.

Through a dim perspective of trees they could glimpse it half a mile away.

Crumbling Georgian. Twisted chimneys. Sagging lintels. Weeds and clods in the guttering like the edge of a turf-bank.

'And she's got twenty-two cats!'

Though it was muttered to the world, the boy knew he had to supply particular comment. Words were like pennies – they had to be picked up and handed back.

'How about kittens, Daddy?'

'I'm including them.'

'When does a kitten become a cat, Daddy?'

'Shut up!'

Stopping, they looked up to the left at a scraggy hill of wind-tattered pine and silver birch.

A lone ash leaned back off the hill, the roots barely holding it in the boggy ground. It looked like a wispy old man unable to walk another step.

Round about them in the plushy trees, pigeons cooed and shot up into the sky with a prayer-book snap of wings. A sparrow-hawk swirled lazily, then hovered, wings fluttering rapidly like a moth at a window.

'That'll be the beggar all right. As sure as there's cotton in cork.'

'The hawk, Daddy?'

'No. The ash. That ash.'

They came out of the wood into a broad expanse of rich pasture, the drive flanked on either side by iron railings.

A huge horse-chestnut stood in the middle of a field,

its massive trunk ringed by a wooden bench. Lady Sarah was sometimes seen sitting there, painting at an easel.

The house loomed closer. His father to give himself courage began to mutter and heap contempt on the Butler-Cootes, going back for inspiration to the days of King James, when they were first planted in the county.

'All forest this one time. From here to Enniskillen in trees. Chopped. Chopped. To get at the rebels. The timber sent to London for their ships and palaces. The people sent to Hell or Connaught. And we have to come bowing and scraping still, for a bit of firewood. Bet your bottom dollar she gives us that oul ash back there!'

Spittle flying he looked furiously about, searching for something to give him offence.

'Damn the lot of them but we'll get even with them yet!'

He was really angry with himself. And that's when he was at his most dangerous. The boy knew when they met Lady Sarah or her steward his face would glow with sweetness and light. His father was only a Sergeant. He had to be polite to his betters.

'What do you think?'

The boy hated being dragged into this conspiracy against the world. And the question was loaded. Wrong answers led to verbal abuse and threats. He hadn't been beaten yet but he feared the moment wasn't far away. If not now, later, if not tomorrow, soon. Every boy in the village got beaten. His turn was bound to come.

'Do you know what I'd do with them, Daddy? I'd stick them to a tree with six-inch nails and set them alight!'

He had learned that going one better usually brought his father back to reality. Being a policeman he was afraid of extremism in others.

'Oh! Oh! Big words in a small mouth. A poor old lady, never did harm to anyone, nailed to a tree?'

'But you said, Daddy, that . . .'

'Never mind what I said!'

To avoid arriving in a useless, self-defeating lather of passion his father slowed down and stopped. The boy went past him, hit a pothole and came to a dead stop. For a moment he balanced in space, then, as he began to keel over, pedalled hard to right himself. Losing direction he careered wildly into the iron railings, the carrier over his back wheel flying backwards and clattering to the ground.

'Now you've done it!'

Picking the carrier up, his father tried to wedge it back into position. The required nuts and flange missing, he attempted to replace them with brute strength and fury. His every finger was a raw-red angry thumb.

'There's a screw missing, Daddy.'

'There is indeed. And a screw loose as well.'

How was it he always had a cutting reply? Where did he find the words?

'Come on, you'll have to carry it. A fine sight you'll make for her ladyship. A carrier being carried.'

The lawns around Coote House were barbered neat,

clean and crew-cut short. A green velvet sea sweeping between bobbing islands of Chinese lanterns, hollyhocks and rich red English roses, they were part of Lady Sarah's pride and joy. Time could ravish her house and life but her lawns, flowers, cats and trees she would defend until her last breath.

At the side of the house the lawn was given over to the game of croquet, a game so alien to the locals they could neither understand it nor pronounce it.

As the boy and his father approached they saw a group of people standing about in sloping angles of inspection, lost from each other in a world of long-handled mallets, wooden balls and hoops stuck like toy railway bridges into the grass.

Men wore straw hats, shirts, flannel trousers and very white shoes.

The boy knew only Protestants wore white shoes.

Women were in thick brogues, thick stockings, tweed skirts, blouses and summer hats.

Lady Sarah, her arthritic back bent, was measuring distances and possibilities.

Straddling the wooden balls, the mallet back between her legs, she suddenly flicked it forward with ferocious decision. With a cluck and click the balls spurted away, then, slowed down by the thick pile on the carpet of grass, rolled lazily to a halt.

The men laughed and one of them burped. Near the gable end of the house stood a small white table with a cloth, jugs and glasses.

'What are they doing, Daddy?'

'Crokee. It's supposed to be a game. You'd better go over and let them know we're here.'

The command with its cunning air of good advice annoyed the boy. He knew his father hadn't the courage or grace to break easily into Lady Sarah's dream-like world.

Still holding the carrier, like a drowning man clutching a straw, he stepped on to the lawn and made for the man nearest to him.

The grass springy under his feet, he had the sensation of swimming out into the lake, the waters getting deeper and more mysterious beneath him.

The strange faces were clean and fresh, the voices English. None of them had noticed his approach.

'Lady Sarah ... Daddy wants you, please.' No one heard him.

He felt ashamed holding the carrier and wanted to throw it away so he wouldn't be seen with it.

After what seemed an age, the burping man turned and looked at him. At first regarding him blankly, then with an exaggerated shifting of eyebrows, popping of eyes and twitching of large moustache, he boomed in jovial surprise, 'I say, Sarah, we've got a little visitor.'

The entire party turned and viewed him. Confronted by such dazzling whiteness he shyly lowered his head. There were holes in his gansey, and his short pants, reduced from an old pair of his father's uniform trousers, were mud-stained.

Lady Sarah playfully raised his chin with her finger and he peered up into her eyes, which were grotesquely

33

distorted by the thick lenses of her spectacles. There was a myth she was on name terms with every child in the village but the boy knew she had no idea who he was.

'Who IS the little poppet?' one of the guests asked.

He pointed to his father, standing stiffly by his bicycle, in the driveway.

'Ah,' Lady Sarah cried, 'the Sergeant.'

Retreating from the pool of smiles and following her he noticed her feet were nearly as big as his father's. The great brogues printed themselves in the lick of lawn dew all the way over to where she was greeted like a dear friend.

'Oh, Lady Sarah, what a charming evening!'

He winced at his father's modulated voice and the affected way he pronounced 'charming'. It sounded like 'chumming'.

Lady Sarah liked his father. In his dark-blue uniform and with his chiselled features he was undeniably handsome. Despite her riches no man had ever married her. It was said that those not put off by her ugliness were soon sent packing by her intelligence.

'How "chumming" to see you,' said his father, 'and it's fresh and well you're looking.'

Lady Sarah giggled and, resting her hand on the sleeve of his tunic, enquired about his health, his wife and the state of the country. Presently he took off his cap. A red line ran along his forehead and his hair was matted in sweat. The effort of keeping up the fawning accent was proving too great a strain. He mopped his brow with a big white handkerchief.

34

'Yes, it is rather humid, would you care for some barley water?'

Declining he came straight to the point and asked for a tree.

'Winter will be upon us before we know.'

Lady Sarah, squinting up at him, stroked the thick black hair on her upper lip and, tapping the croquet mallet on the ground for inspiration, remembered there was a tree in danger of falling round by the lake. It was halfway up a hill surrounded by silver birch.

'Andy, I call it,' she said, 'it's an ash.'

She would get her steward to mark it so it could be easily identified.

His father's face was a mask of interest and gratitude but behind the glazed eyes the boy knew the turmoil of rage, sarcasm and malice shunting round his head.

'Thank you, Lady Sarah, thank you so very much.'

Getting on their bikes they rode homeward and as soon as they were out of earshot his father started.

'Well, the oul vixen! The world wouldn't believe it! But she's got a Christian name for every single tree! Andy! I told you, didn't I? I knew that was the one she'd fob off on us! Well, feck her! And her seed, breed and generation into the bargain! And their bloody oul crokee as well. Andy!'

When they reached the hill they stopped and looked up at the ash which to the boy looked even more withered and forlorn than before. Andy wasn't a particularly attractive name at the best of times and it seemed to him to be peculiarly suited to the lonely weakling tree.

'Well, God blast you, but there's only about two months burning in you if that, which means we'll have to come back and start the whole business all over again!'

'Andy Ash,' said the boy quietly.

'It's no joke! And it wasn't a joke either seeing them crokee players sniggering at you, standing there with your carrier in front of you like a squirrel holding a nut!'

Seeing the black rage in his father's face, he knew a syllable uttered in his defence could end with a raw-red slap on the ear, a fist maybe in the face, a kick even. He'd seen it happening to his friends.

On the rest of the journey home he stayed well clear and that night went early to bed saying his prayers extra loud so his father could hear him in the kitchen and think him far too pious for a beating.

Next morning he was told he had to stay at home to help cut down the tree.

'He's too young to help,' protested his mother, 'and anyway why can't you do it on Saturday when he doesn't have to miss school?'

'I'm doing it today and that's all!'

'Are you up to something?' enquired his mother crossly.

'No,' replied his father.

'Then why the rush to cut it down today?'

His father smiled but didn't reply. They watched as he sliced into a boiled egg, the top of which he gave to the boy.

After breakfast he wheeled out his father's bicycle

then went back into the shed to get the implements needed for tree-felling.

The shed was a long narrow dark affair and so cluttered with gardening tools, wheelbarrows, bicycle wheels, pots and pans, tilley lamps, Primus stoves, ropes, galvanised sheets and buckets, the boy was the only one able to negotiate the tangled chaos.

His mother had dubbed it the 'American Collection', because one day when his father had attempted to bring order to it, he kicked over a pile of empty paint cans and shouted angrily, 'I wish to God I'd gone to America years ago!'

The boy groped about in the dark searching for a hessian sack and knew he had found the right one when he heard the dull clink of heavy wedges. He humped, hopped and dragged them towards the light and his father's waiting hand.

'Get down that cross-cut now.'

He reached to where the saw rested upside down on two nails. As if having life of its own it leaped from his grasp, whanging against a stack of oil drums, tumbling them over with a doomy clatter.

'Easy, easy!'

Round the front of the barracks his mother watched as they loaded the gear on to his father's bicycle. The wedges sat on the carrier and secured to the crossbar was an axe, a sledgehammer and a slash-hook. The boy had the cross-cut and round his neck carried a rope. His mother put a bottle of tea into his father's pocket and they set off for the demesne entrance.

Soon they were deep in the lullaby silence of the wood.

He liked carrying the cross-cut. It had two shiny hardwood handles and in the middle a smooth brassy solder, brazed there after being snapped by a falling tree. As he walked it bounced against his thigh and he imagined it was a bow with himself the arrow poised and ready for flight.

A beam of sunlight eased down through a tattered curtain of low cloud. It shone through the trees and brazed a small patch of open ground a bright golden colour just like the soldered spot on the cross-cut.

'Look what's coming,' muttered his father, as Mickey the gatehouse simpleton came towards them, a bundle of twigs on his back.

'Grand day, grand day, grand day now,' he shouted to them, a huge grin bandaged on his lardy face.

'Lady Sarah gone to town?' enquired his father.

'Oh aye, oh aye, oh aye. Every Thursday.' He winked at the boy and stuck his tongue out: a poor fool compelled to confirm his idiocy at every encounter.

Going round by the lake they disturbed a heron which rose in panic before them, desperately flapping its spindly body into the air.

'Greedy blaggards, the same herons.'

'Why, Daddy?'

'They gulp the fish in one end and to stop it coming straight out the other, they sit their bums on a stone.'

His father didn't have the imagination to invent fantastic tales. The truth in his mouth was lurid enough.

'Tell us how you won the medal for bravery, Daddy, ah go on.'

'You've heard it often enough. When we've the tree down and chopped up I might tell you.'

They came to the ash. Lady Sarah's steward had already marked it with a whitewashed circle. In contemptuous silence his father stared up at it. He still held on to his bicycle and when the boy went to remove the wedges from the carrier, in surly anger rounded on him.

'What are you doing? That's not the one!'

'Yes it is, Daddy. Andy.'

'No it's not. Our one is further along.'

'No it's not. This is the one.'

'I tell you it's not!'

His eyes were glazed, his face cranky as the cross-cut teeth. He looked at the boy, challenging him to contradict. In the silence the flies buzzed round the peak of his cap.

'But I thought, Daddy, that . . .' He could hear his heart beating as panic furred his tongue. His father was in the grip of some mad, mysterious plot. Looking up once more towards the ash he knew it was the one. The white circle marked it out even more from the surrounding healthy trees. A scald crow landed on it and with a melancholy screech proclaimed the truth for all the world to hear.

'It is the one, Daddy. I know it is!'

'Now you don't know everything. Come on.' He puffed his lips, winked and smiled, trying to soften the boy, lull him, make him an accomplice. They walked on, pausing occasionally to look up at the majestic trees flanking the drive. As he stared into the huge branches, his father had one side of his lower lip gripped in his teeth.

They came to a great elm, big as a circus tent. His father looked at it, stroking his chin, pondering, biting his lip. The boy with horror in his heart began to realise what it was they were about to do. His father, furtively looking up and down the drive, circled the tree, grunted at it, touched it with his fingers, then walked on. The boy was relieved.

'Oh yes, they chopped the woods to get at the rebels! It's time the rebels chopped back.'

Sick with worry, he knew his father was going to cut down the wrong tree. On purpose. It had nothing to do with rebels. It was out of pure greed and a wild hope that Lady Sarah wouldn't notice. But the boy knew and everyone in the village knew, Lady Sarah would miss a leaf, never mind one of the great trees along the drive to Coote House.

How could his father dare? If discovered how could he brazen it out? They stopped beside a magnificent copper beech. His father immediately growled approval as if looking at a thoroughbred animal.

'This is the one all right. We'll knock her back into that clearing there. Perfect.'

'It's not this one, Daddy. Honest. It's not.'

Throwing the bag of wedges to the ground his father shouted angrily, 'Get me that axe, you pup you, and don't be annoying me. If I say it's the one that's enough.

It is the one! A beech. I know rightly this is the one. And you know it too!'

The meaning hidden in the last few words hung heavily on the dull air. If they were found out he would be blamed. He was powerless. And his mother at home, probably peeling potatoes into the aluminium basin and happily humming to herself.

'What if Lady Sarah comes along?'

'So? She gave it to us, didn't she?'

'No, she didn't!'

'Anyway, she always goes to town on Thursdays. We'll have her felled, trimmed, sawn and chopped before she's back.'

So that's why it had to be today. He had it planned. Poor Mickey the simpleton had confirmed her absence.

He tried to circle the trunk with his arms but couldn't. And the topmost branches seemed to be sticking into the clouds.

'It's too big, Daddy. We'll never do it.'

But his father was no longer listening. Giving the trunk a whack with the axe he lifted the cross-cut to the gash. Slowly the teeth tore into the tree. The boy did no more than steady his end as his father, on one knee, back and neck bent sideways, drove the saw over and back with a powerful urgent rhythm. Sawdust pumped out into the ground in bloody arcs.

Already the boy's wrists ached. His father had a cold passion which could burn at a task for hours nonstop. His iron will and ruthless strength, which grew more brutish as the minutes passed, would destroy the soul of a saint. Each time the saw stuck he grunted angrily and squealed as if the tree and the cross-cut were ganging up on him. Already the boy's nerves were fraying.

His father loved working in the open air. He loved felling trees. He knew heavyweight boxers did it when training for title fights. His favourite song was Phil Harris singing 'Woodman Spare That Tree'. The only poem he knew began with the line, 'I think that I shall never see a poem as lovely as a tree'. He loved trees. He couldn't help chopping them down. He was beyond understanding.

Withdrawing the saw, his father got the axe and above the cut began to chop out the fall-hole. This huge bite taken out of the trunk would eventually force the tree to fall in a certain direction. With each axe-blow a thick curl of wood flew out until the ground seemed scattered with pale lumps of pink flesh.

A copper leaf fell gently to the ground.

This time they would carry on cutting until the tree toppled down. It had stood for over a hundred years. Lady Sarah loved it. Only a short time before when interviewed in the *Anglo-Celt* she said that apart from oak her favourite species was the copper beech.

The boy felt they were committing murder. The swoosh and rip of the cross-cut silenced all the birds. The sun came out and shone on them like a flashlamp on two thieves in the night.

Every move his father made had a crouched urgency. The job had to be done before Lady Sarah got back from town. He wasn't afraid of being caught by her steward.

Her steward was an Englishman cashiered from the Army for homosexuality. There was a file on him in the barracks. And he wasn't afraid of the workmen. They were Catholics.

Kneeling on the sack, to stop the damp penetrating his knees, and in a lather of sweat he cursed the flies that buzzed his face, the braces which kept slipping from one shoulder and the boy who was almost fainting with fatigue.

'I must have a rest, Daddy.'

'No, damn you! Not till she's down!'

The cross-cut tore slowly into the belly of the tree. It made a deep swishing sound. The sound his mother's nails made when she scratched his back.

'Who the hell . . . ?'

A tall man approached along the drive. He wore knicker-bockers and on his head a deer-stalker hat.

'It's one of Lady Sarah's visitors.'

The man nodded, smiled and in a plummy accent said, 'Hot work, eh?'

His father had to stop to acknowledge him. The boy's head sunk to his chest in relief. He rubbed his wrists and stood up to stretch his back. His wrists were thin as the legs of the heron dangling over the lake.

'Enjoying your holiday?'

'Oh yes, always do.'

'That's the stuff.'

The cross-cut sagged in the tree, the golden solder sunk in the ever-deepening cut.

The man unable to hold the unfriendly stare walked on.

43

'I've seen some quare hawks in me time but that one takes the biscuit.'

The boy laughed, hoping to delay his father starting again.

'They wouldn't go round in England dressed up like that. But as soon as they set foot here out comes the Sherlock Holmes attire and begod they think they're Lord and Lady Muck!'

The boy laughed again, but couldn't further delay the inevitable moment.

'Get hold.'

'I want to pee, Daddy.'

'No. Get hold.'

The sawdust pumped out again and the noise swished and sighed through the deep sweet wood.

'Blast.' The saw was stuck.

They tapped a small wedge into the slit, easing the weight of the tree from the saw. They cut further in and, as the pressure increased, drove in bigger wedges. The soldered repair was the problem. Though smooth it wasn't flush, catching easily, usually when it was the boy's turn to pull. He hated that golden mark now. Why couldn't his father buy a new cross-cut? Why not a chainsaw? Even a second-hand one. No. Heavyweight boxers were never photographed with chainsaws. Besides, they cost a fortune and his father was so mean he'd resist for ages having to buy a new battery for his bicycle-lamp. He'd heat and re-heat the old one in the oven to prolong its lingering life.

At last they passed the halfway mark and the weight

of the tree began to tilt towards the fall-hole. The pressure eased, his father drove the saw to and fro at a frantic pace. His will whetted his strength and gave him furious power.

'Come on! Come on! Topple, you beggar!'

A wedge fell out. The tree was beginning to go. The boy glanced up at it. He was worried. What if it fell on them?

'Run back that way when I tell you to!'

The tree was quivering. Nervous ripples ran through it. Like when a horse shivers its flesh against hornets.

His father looked up into the branches with a calculating eye.

'Just another bit now. Good boy.'

The tree creaked, groaned but still held. His father got the sledgehammer and drove the big wedge further in.

'Look out in case she kicks back at us.'

The boy was terrified. His father looked worried. The tree was immense. Their movements were slower now, tense: gently letting the saw nibble ever deeper, tapping the wedge in after it.

The sweat poured down their faces and hung at the end of their noses. Their clothes stuck like damp poultice to their skins. His father smiled at him. It was a smile of encouragement. He was proud of his father. Only a great man could dare knock down so great a tree. And he had helped. He loved his father.

They stopped sawing and listened to the tree. Starting again, his father murmured gently to it, calming it. Like a butcher with a sheep.

'That's the girl. Easy, easy.'

Suddenly a terrifying, tearing, bone-snapping crack rang out like a gun-shot.

'She's going.'

Branches quaking, the huge tree tilted, twisted and, fighting to stay upright, grabbed at a neighbouring tree but, bowing to its fate, keeled over and with a creaking goodbye-sigh rushed to the earth with a thunderous hurricane crash. The boy felt the shock waves in his feet and saw the light flood in to the space where the tree had stood. Overhead the sky was bigger.

His father grinned.

'It's massive, Daddy. It's bigger than a ship.'

'It'll see us through the winter, thank God.'

As the boy skipped round the tree the enormity of what they'd done struck home. The shield and tangle of bough, branch and leaf looked impenetrable. It had taken them over two hours to knock it; it would take them the rest of the day at least to trim, lop, saw and chop it. Certainly they would not be done by the time Lady Sarah returned. And even if they were she could not possibly miss the pile of timber awaiting collection.

'How will we get it home?'

'Barney Smith's tractor and trailer. Tomorrow evening.'

Tomorrow? Evening? It was mad. Ridiculous. Lady Sarah was bound to find out.

Tired out he sat on the tree-stump beside his father and had alternate swigs at the bottle of cold tea.

Hearing a noise he turned his head and instantly his

body and blood went cold. Approaching along the drive at the wheel of her Wolsey car was Lady Sarah.

Time stopped dead. His father gave a strangled groan and his face iced over in hatred. They were caught like rats in a trap.

The car crunched to a halt. He was terrified in case his father did something desperate and was all the more amazed when he saw him smiling and in high good nature waving to Lady Sarah as she, horror-stricken, stepped on to the drive. Wearing a peculiar 1920s hat and a flapping plastic mac she dismissed his father's greeting and staggered towards the tree.

'What have you done, Sergeant, what have you done?' she wailed. 'You have killed one of my beauties!' Grabbing and clutching the stricken branches she buried herself in the copper leaves. The boy could hear her sobs but couldn't see where she was.

'Oh, Beatrice, Beatrice my beauty, how has this occurred?'

His father winked.

'What's wrong, Lady Sarah, what seems to be the problem?'

'The problem,' she replied, stepping from the tree, 'is you have murdered the wrong tree.' Behind the thick lenses of her spectacles her eyes were tiny red dots of dismay.

'Oh no, we haven't, have we?' howled his father, his face a dancing mask of pantomime surprise. 'Good Lord I can't believe it. Are you sure, Lady Sarah?'

'Oh yes, I'm sure all right. I gave you a weakling ash, not this!'

Suddenly he turned to the boy and made as if to strike him.

'Didn't I tell you it wasn't this one? I told you all along!'

The boy hung his head in shame and didn't dare look at Lady Sarah because he knew she knew his father lied.

'I'll do anything I can by way of reparation, anything. I remember you saying the name, Andy. I think that's what confused me. That and the boy. Beech is no good to me anyway. It's a poor burner. A weakling ash is exactly what I wanted, Lady Sarah.'

He stalked over and back, feeling his brow, looking at the sky, at the ground, almost on the point of tears, imploring her to allow him to make amends.

'One thing you cannot do is put it back up where it was this morning.'

There was a hint of hoping for miracles in her voice.

Once more he blamed the boy and made a run at him as if to hit him. Darting out of his way he went close to Lady Sarah and looked into her eyes. She knew.

Turning away she faced the dead Beatrice and with her frail hand plucked a copper leaf. Resting it on her fingers like a clot of blood, she held it to her mouth and nose and sighed as if kissing goodbye to a loved one. 'Beatrice, Beatrice, you were my father's favourite,' she whispered.

Tears welled in the boy's eyes. Lady Sarah looked very old, very sad and a little frightened. She owned the great demesne, employed many people, was kowtowed to in every town and village along the Border but up against his father was just a lonely spinster, powerless to command. He was the Sergeant. She needed him to protect her property. The law was hers but it was on his word it was carried out.

His father stopped moving about, stopped cringing and with a steady gaze looked down at her.

The sweat dripping from his face, his chest heaving in his open shirt, his big thumbs twitching at his braces, his great booted feet straddling the driveway, the cold appealing look in his pale-blue eyes were all too much for gentle hearts to cope with.

Getting into her car she spoke softly, her pride hurt, her spirit shocked. 'You may as well finish what you so cruelly started.'

'Well, that's the only damn thing we can do now, Lady Sarah.'

Hours later as they rode home past Andy, though his body ached his soul raged rampant at the conquering smirk on his father's face.

LINO

A WHITE EYE OF PILL sat on the sewing machine. His father hated it. He couldn't understand why he suddenly had to start taking it. He was told it was to regulate his heart. But only a few months previously the doctor had told him his heart was sound as a bell. The boy watched him staring at the pill, trying to understand why he had to swallow it.

The boy knew the secret. It gave him power over his father. But only in his head. He could never say it aloud. It annoyed him that he and his mother had to burden themselves with it. Why shouldn't his father be told? It was his problem! Why was his mother always placating him, cosseting him? Actually protecting him from himself! It was infuriating. But the boy knew if the secret escaped from the barracks it would soon reach the Authorities in Dublin and that would mean disaster.

But could any future be worse than life in this Border

Station, where the rains fell red on to the rocky bleeding hills and the damp nights closed in on them grey as blankets?

Wet, cobbling days were the worst. His father changed into dungarees, brought his boot box into the kitchen and using the sewing machine as a work base proceeded to slash, hammer, sew, groan and curse his way through the afternoon.

He hated indoor jobs forced on him by the rain and now on top of that he had to contend with that eye of pill placed where he couldn't avoid seeing it.

The boy watched him as he sat whipping a length of thread across his thigh, rolling wax over it, puffing his cheeks and lips out in time with the crude rhythm of his movements. His mother hated the puffing. The sharp blasts disturbed and threatened. Penned in by the weather and furious at his own awkwardness he tried to revenge himself even on the silent air.

'Haven't you taken that pill yet?' said his mother.

'No! No, I haven't! Are you blind?' roared his father.

His mother began to cry, the tears rolling down her cheeks, lingering along her jawbone before dropping like rain on to her new white blouse.

Her sobs could knock bridges, snap trees, flitter the boy's jumping feathery heart.

His father puffed, groaned, belted the anvil and bared his teeth.

'Bad cess to this blasted weather!'

The boot box was bunged with bits of leather, old heels, awls, knives, rasps, needles and tiny nails in a tin

Gold Flake cigarette box. There was one piece of good leather which was kept rolled up and tied round the middle with binder twine. When unrolled it was suntan shiny on one side, rough and fluffy to the touch on the other. To soften it his father soaked it, then beat it on the last. The hammer ringed itself in perfect circles all over the hide.

'Where does glue come from?'

'Cows' hooves, Daddy.'

'What are rosary beads made from?'

'Cows' horns, Daddy.'

'What's leather?'

'Cow skin, Daddy.'

'Don't keep saying Daddy.'

'Yes, Daddy. I mean no, Daddy.'

'Jesus! What's offal?'

'Cows' guts.'

'Good boy. We're fed and shod by her and in India she's sacred. In Ireland we pray with bits of her.'

'Were you ever in India, Daddy?'

'No. I've never been further than square one and the arsehole of nowhere!'

Drawing the thread through the grip of his wax-filled fist it began to glisten and stiffen like a dead eel.

'You thread this needle, with your young eyes. Mine are going.'

'You'd see the Queen on a five-pound note, all right,' said his mother.

'Only whilst handing it over to you!'

The thread was sticky, the end fine as a thorn.

53

When he felt the ball of wax it was hot from his father's hand and criss-crossed with lines.

The night was waxy, his mother's skin as warm. He slept with his mother. Their room by day was ordinary but by night a cave of mystery.

A candle had the power to dance a wardrobe against a wall, grow thorns into blood, burn black night like a fire through coal. Jesus was the picture and the oily blood hissed out of the burning heart. A shadow of a man stood in front of the wardrobe, looking down at him. He was tall, pale and wore a brown hat.

'Who is that man, Mammy?'

'What man, darling? Go to sleep.'

The candle had light and magic but no heat. His mother's body was fleecy warm. He went soft in her arms, running to hot liquid, lapping inside her soupy skin, dreaming into her smiling bony head. Pulling her nightdress open at the neck, with calm lips he searched her breast.

'No, like a good boy.'

'Mammy.'

'You're too big any more.'

'I love you, love you, Mammy.'

Suckling hayfield smells and warm waves of basting heat came from her and rolled him down towards melting sleep.

The wardrobe flickered, damp shadows distempered themselves to the flaking walls and away out under the ocean sky a motorbike sped along the Border road, its high-pitched whine threading back along the night like a cobweb floating on the breeze.

One night he awoke to see his father standing in the middle of the room, one hand on his mother's neck, the other holding up his pyjamas. His mother's night-dress was round her thighs and then his father put his arms round her and trembling like leaves they stood there as the candle danced them round the room and up across the ceiling. He tightly shut his eyes and lay still in the moaning dark until he heard his mother at the jug and basin.

His father had gone back to his room. He slept alone in a single bed. The bed was iron, hard, high and for blankets had layers of police greatcoats. The room smelt of ointments, medicines and holy poverty. Under the bed was a pooley-pot and a big black box containing letters, documents, bank books and the medal won for bravery. Looped over the bar of the bed-head was a rosary beads with a crucifix which slid open. In a tiny recess of the bottom half was a piece of wood that had touched a piece of wood from the cross that Jesus died on.

The day the new lino was delivered as they knelt that evening at prayer the boy saw a cockroach speed across the floor and under the bridge of his father's ankle and upturned boot.

It was the following night the secret came crawling out from the depths of his father's brain. And it would forever repeat itself unless he took the pill.

'Sitting there, staring into space . . . what are you at?'
'Nothing, Daddy.'
'Hand me that boot.'
His boots were big as coal-scuttles. Clowns' boots.

Police boots. His feet were cheesy, the toes long and corn-horny. His mother had to pare them with a safety razor. Holding his leg under his knee he stuck his foot up on her lap and grimaced as the rinds of hard skin collected on her dress.

The boy took up the bits and tossed them on the hot range. He liked to watch them frazzle, twist and smoke. Souls in Hell did the same thing and if you didn't believe that how could you believe in Santa Claus? Your soul was inside you, like your brain. But if anything crawled out of it, it could, luckily, only be seen by God. Your soul looked like a side of meat hanging in the butchers. Raw white so stains could clearly be seen by Angels. A sin tasted like suet and smelt sweet and sour like butter-milk. Sins were ugly thumbmarks on your suety soul. And there was no white eye of pill to cure them.

Over his mother's bed hung a picture of Jesus. The eyes were screwed up in black agony towards the crown of thorns that spiked the head. Tiny apple seeds of blood wept down the face. At night he hid from the sight under the blankets and tried thinking of sweets and football until his mother came to bed. But all the time he knew it was hanging above him in the dark.

In his father's cobbling box were studs, each one having three sharp prongs for sticking into leather soles. Segs, his father called them. They came on cards with a coloured picture of a cross-legged leprecaun sitting at an anvil mending shoes.

The leprecaun and Jesus were the only pictures in the house.

'Hand me that awl! What's the welt?'

'I don't know!'

'And you don't care. It's that bit there between upper and sole.'

His mother had stopped crying and was sitting looking out at the rain pelting into the panes and running in frantic gushes over the edge of the sill.

The white eye of pill still sat on the sewing machine.

Out the back the hen-house door banged open and shut and on the big tin bath hanging on the gable wall the rain drummed deeply crazy music.

In the summer, each first Friday of the month his father filled the bath and, naked, squatted in the cold water scrubbing himself from head to toe. From the barrel his mother poured buckets of water over him and they laughed at his shouts of protest.

His skin was white and pimply with the cold. His mother didn't approve of his hearty display of nakedness. She was afraid farmers delivering milk to the nearby creamery would see him.

'Do you want to get in?'

'No, Daddy.'

'I bet you don't.'

Drying himself he breathed hard, sucking the air through his teeth towards the roof of his mouth, making a whooshing rattling sound like a train gathering speed.

He hung his uniform on the cross-tree which was used for sawing timber. The cross-tree was like everything his father made – crude, lopsided but somehow indestructible.

Standing in baggy underpants, staring at the sky, he suddenly turned and caught the boy peering at him from round the corner of the sheds.

'Who do you love the best – me or mum?'

'Both.'

'I loved my mother the best. Your granny.'

It was hard to imagine him having a mother.

'What was Granny like?'

Pondering, he put on his vest, his blue shirt, his trousers, hitching the braces over his shoulders with a grunt. Then he donned his tunic. His greying hair was wet, tousselled, his big white feet bare.

'She smoked a pipe and was better than most men. We were all born in a mud hut but when the British set up the Congested District Board we got a house. Real walls. Real slates. We didn't have enough furniture to fill the few rooms. That'll give you some idea, me bucko!'

He loved it when his father made him feel he belonged to a tough race of men.

'Come here.'

Holding the boy's face with one hand he peered into his eyes.

'Good men always love their mother the best. You'll find I won't mind.'

'I do love her the best.'

'Why did you say "both" then?'

Like segs, the fingers gripped his jawbone, then slowly slipped to his chin where they rested in a stiff bunch.

'Go into the kitchen and come back with an orange.'

They sat at the back of the barracks on a rickety form,

his father slicing the orange into quarters with his penknife. Wiping the juicy blade along his tongue he handed one quarter of the fruit to the boy. They spat the pips into the soapy water of the bath and with bared teeth his father ripped at the pithy skin.

A blackbird landed on the wall but on seeing them flew screeching away.

'Bad cess to the same blackbird.'

'Why, Daddy?'

'Why? The brazen beggars destroy the strawberries, that's why!'

When he wasn't staring at you his father's eyes were restless, searching. He was always on the look-out for criminals. Except in this part of the world there weren't any. Only smugglers, IRA men and farmers who allowed donkeys to walk the roads unshod. Smugglers he wouldn't and IRA men he couldn't catch, so he had to demean himself with the donkeys, bicycles with no rear lights and neighbours fighting over trespassing cattle.

'Donkeys and bicycle pumps! Me! Who worked on three murder cases in me day!' With martyr's face and agonised intensity he spoke to the boy.

'One good murder, that's all I ask. One good murder!'

'Tell us one of your murders, Daddy, please.'

'No. Some other time.'

'Ah, go on.'

Biting his lower lip, eyes narrowing for memories, he stared into the bath. Bits of orange wedged his teeth.

'Blew his brother's brains out with a shotgun, he did. The sister was implicated as well. Over a will. A piece of land left by their father. So poor a snipe would have to wear wellingtons to land on it. Long, greasy, balding hair he had and a beard. In court he wore a big Sacred Heart badge on his chest. To impress the jury. When the judge donned the Black Cap he started squealing like a rat ... "You will be taken from your cell," says the judge, "on the morning of the 4th April, to where the hangman will place a hempen rope about your neck, the knot at the butt of your lug, and on the morning gong of seven the trapdoor lever pulled and through the air your soul shall fly as down below your body twists in dangling agony of death. Amen!"'

Reaching forward he gripped the handle of the bath and with a twist of his wrist tipped it over. The grey water rushed along the grass flattening it, matting it down, soaking into the earth with bubbly sighs.

His mother rapped at the window.

'You haven't a styme of sense telling him them old stories. Frightening the life out of him!'

Words or pictures. They were the same. They frightened in equal measure. Words *were* pictures. He could see the poor hanged man slowly swivelling, above him the grey smile of the hangman rubbing his hands at a job well done.

Above his bed hung the bleeding face of Jesus. He too had long greasy hair and a beard. In his mind the two became one. Hanged, crucified – it was a shocking end to those who went against the law. And in Butlershill his father was the law. He had the silver buttons to prove it, with the G and S of Garda Siochana linked like snakes.

He had the baton, the handcuffs with key dangling on green ribbon, the chevrons on his sleeve and below everything his big black boots. But now he possessed a secret to upend all that power. Unable to stop worrying about it he feared the secret was possessing him. He hated it. It was too much to hide and he hoped his father would somehow prise it from him. But he had promised his mother!

'What he doesn't know won't trouble him,' she had said.

His father began hammering tiny nails into his boot then turned and looked at him. He could feel the magnet eyes pulling his thoughts out. He forced himself to look away. His mother winked at him.

Suddenly his father lashed out at the pill.

His mother left the kitchen.

It had landed on the blue lino, just by the leg of the table. When they first came to live in the barracks the floor was bare concrete. His father wouldn't buy a roll of lino and his mother couldn't as she hadn't a penny to her name. Many years before, the walls had been painted grey and green and in a tiled recess an old range wheezed smoke every time the wind blew down the chimney. Repairs and decoration his father insisted were the responsibility of the Board of Works in Dublin. His father wrote to them but they ignored his letters. One he fired off commenced – 'Dear Bow-Wow, You may think we're all dogs but no longer are we prepared to live in this kennel!' For weeks he chuckled at his own sarcasm but it had no practical effect.

'Unless you live in a Round Tower or a Georgian

mansion you'll get nothing done for you in this country! I wish to God I'd gone to America years ago!'

'Well, I wish you had,' shouted his mother, 'all I'm asking is a roll of lino. The place is a disgrace. I'm ashamed to bring anyone in!'

At last his father relented.

There being only two shops of any consequence in Butlershill, neither possessing linoleum, it had to be purchased in Cavan town. He and his mother journeyed there on the train.

His mother wore her one good suit. A dark-blue pinstriped jacket with wide lapels and matching skirt. It gave off a whiff of perfume and moth-balls. Of her three hats she selected the one with the diamond pin. She stood looking at herself in the mirror and finally decided not to wear her fox-fur. It hung in the wardrobe, brown, sharp-snouted with dark dead button-eyes.

He loved watching her wash, powder and dress. All the time she looked at herself in the glass, even when she reached for the soap or the Ponds vanishing cream. Her movements were soft, gentle and putting on her lipstick they both laughed when she made her lips go gummy over her teeth like an old woman.

He held her gold watch and when she was ready she let him fasten it about her wrist.

'God be with ye,' shouted his father as they set out for the railway station.

On the platform waiting for the train he was so excited he had to run to the urinal behind the ticket office. The urinal was Victorian in design, constructed of decorated metal panels green-painted and black where you pissed. He stood beside a man wearing a British Army greatcoat. The man was small with jet-black hair and a pencil-thin moustache.

'You're the Sergeant's son, aren't you? Well, I'm ex-Private Jimmy Kelly. Do you want to see the bullet holes in me belly?'

'Not now, thank you.'

As the train approached, the ground began to tremble. Jimmy Kelly picking up his bag, a shotgun and a brace of dead rabbits went out singing merrily – 'We're going to hang King Farouk By his ballocks from a hook.'

The train looked huge alongside the tiny platform and slightly comical. The engine and coal-tender pulling the three carriages were facing the wrong way round. From the guard's van a big red-haired man with a whistle and green flag shouted to the station master that there was trouble with the turn-table at Clones.

'We'll be going backwards and forwards at the same time,' said Jimmy Kelly, 'that's why this country's been at a standstill for years.'

He got into their compartment and sat opposite them pulling at his ear, the lobe of which was very thick and the colour of nicotine.

'They weren't liars who said you were a fine-lookin' woman.'

'Words are cheap,' replied his mother.

'It's the only thing is.'

'Which I suppose,' said his mother, 'is why poor men won't shut up.'

A whistle blew and with ferocious hissing, belching, panting, the mighty engine of the GNR backed out for Cavan town.

'GNR. Going Nowhere Remarkable,' said Jimmy Kelly.

'Do you want us to laugh now or can we wait 'til later?' said his mother.

'You've got an ojus sharp tongue. They say what looks sweetest is often sourest.'

'In that case, God help us, you must be as sweet as sugar.'

His mother laughed heartily, enjoying the banter.

The dead rabbits lay on the floor. Blood smirked their mouths and the big eyes frozen open in fear stared at the boy's feet.

'What's on in Cavan today? You must be buying something.'

'None of your business, Jimmy.'

'We're buying lino,' said the boy.

His mother nudged him and Jimmy Kelly roared laughing, his head going up and down almost to his knees, his whole body swaying with the train as it pounded through the cutting dug out from Reilly's hill.

'I've been out since seven this morning, hunting.'

'It's well for you.'

'You have to earn a few shillings someway.'

'You're not short of shillings. With your British Army pension and not a thing the matter with you.'

'Not a thing the matter with me? Not a thing the matter with me? Do you want to see the bullet holes in me belly?'

He angrily grabbed his shirt and was about to pull it from his trousers when the train hooted and slowed down.

He jumped up, grabbed his bag, gun and the dead rabbits, opened the carriage door and hopped out. He was right beside his house at a level crossing. He and his elderly mother operated the gates against oncoming road traffic for which they received from the Great Northern Railway free accommodation, travel and a few pounds a year.

'Not a thing wrong with him,' said his mother, waving out, 'the British government must be terrible eejits, good luck to him.'

In the town they made for the Bank of Ireland where his father had an account. The manager attended them. He wore a white shirt with sleeves down to his knuckles and had a pair of spectacles saddled on the end of his big blue whiskey nose.

The oak counter smelt of polish and from the ceiling a chandelier showered light on the diamond-patterned floor tiles and flashed at the pin in his mother's hat.

'And how are things,' asked the manager, 'out in the wilds?'

'Very tame. Especially the men. How are they in here?'

'I wouldn't know the answer to that one,' he laughed.

'And I don't want to find out,' said his mother.

The manager laughed again and, licking his thumb, counted out the money.

Away from the barracks his mother had a laughing face and a light step. People loved her. He was proud walking beside her, the only one in the whole world holding her hand.

They went into a tea-room and ordered bread and jam sandwiches and a pot of tea. Then they had a glass of lemonade with ice cream in it. This they sipped through straws and ate with long-handled spoons. And when it was all gone his mother ordered more.

The waitress smiled at them and said, 'Is it going to rain, do you think?'

His mother smiled back and said, 'Well, if it doesn't it won't be for the want of trying.'

On the counter was a big shiny tea-urn, the water chugging inside it, wisps of steam escaping out the top. Each table had red oil-cloth and on a wall hung a picture of Palermo, Sicily.

His mother, reaching over, patted down his hair and tightened the knot in his tie.

How did she always smell so sweet, ripe and warm? How was she always soft and why was his father always hard? She was honey, he was water. She was milk, he was skim. She was straw, he was stubble. She was hay, he was thistle. She was feathers, he was bone. And he himself was in between the two of them, wanting to be like her but knowing he looked like him. His reflection in the mirror on the tea-room wall spelt it out. 'Spitting image of your father!' Pictures were words.

In the hardware store an assistant showed them the rolls of lino stacked in a vertical jumble in a corner of the shop. When he tossed each one down they hit the floor with a dull slap and sprout of dust.

'This one here now, missus, I'm telling you it's as good as carpet and ten times cheaper. Almost. I've one meself the very same in the bedroom.'

'It's for the kitchen I want it,' said his mother.

'Oh, no bother, you can put this one down anywhere. Hens coming in now, pigs, the dog, boots . . . she'll never wear out. Last you a lifetime it will, so it will.'

His mother winked to the boy and when the assistant realised they weren't farm people he began to call his mother 'madam'.

His mother inspected every single roll, brushing the glossy surface with her fingers. Finally she chose the first one – the blue.

'What do you think?'

'It's very nice, Mammy. It's nicer than the one with the yellow stripes anyway.' For a horrible moment it looked as if his mother was going to buy the yellow roll.

They paid at a counter which ran the whole length of the shop. Above it was a cash pulley system of wires, elastic bands and handle, propelling wooden cups to a central cash office and which came zinging back with the change and receipt.

'We had one the very same in Ballina,' said his mother.

They left the shop, the assistant promising delivery in 'two days or a week at the latest'.

His mother's people had owned the biggest shop and bakery in the West of Ireland. But through drink and brothers fighting, it had been signed away.

'Poor Mama, she never knew. He used to beat us with stair-rods.'

'Who?'

'Dada.'

'Why?'

'Temper. Temper, drink and badness. RIP.'

Hand in hand they went up the steps and into St Felim's Cathedral where they lit two candles and in the pew nearest the doors sat praying. His mother never knelt. Under her nylon stockings the boy could see the lumpy bandages supporting the veins which ripped through her legs like blue barbed wire.

All around the walls were faces of pious suffering. Like the picture over his bed. Like his father bent over the cobbler's last, in a tense grip of self-inflicted agony.

In the ranks of holy flames the candles were already trickling snotty grease, the burning tongues speaking bravely against the vast doom of the gloomy church.

He had lit his candle for the dead rabbits, the fox in the wardrobe and in thanksgiving that the barracks was a bungalow and therefore hadn't any stair-rods.

Walking to the railway station they could smell pigs. Rearing and killing swine was the main industry of the town and surrounding farms. The odour was so acute the boy spat out the tainted air. They were glad of the fusty smell of the station waiting-room and the tang of Jeyes fluid scrubbed into the bare floorboards. The boards were so worn with use, the nails along the joists shone through like studs in a boot.

A man had pulled up a bench in front of the empty

fireplace and, elbows on knees and fists at the side of his head, propelled spits through the gaps in the grate. He wore a brown hat, brown boots and a Crombie overcoat. An ashplant leant against his leg. Scabs of cow-dung flecked his trousers.

'A cattle-dealer,' whispered his mother, 'they're the boys with the spondulicks.'

He turned and looked at them. His face was round and red as rhubarb, his mouth stained with porter.

'Be Jasus if you don't mind me sayin' so, missus, but you must have been an ojus fine heifer in your day.'

'When asses meet, compliments fly!' replied his mother.

'If I'm an ass you're another so.' He spat into the fireplace. The spit gathered black as it slipped down the sooty fireback.

Outside the train thundered to a stop.

A man shouted, 'Ballyhaise, Butlershill, Clones, Monaghan. Change at Ballyhaise for Belturbet.'

'Belturbet,' growled the cattle-dealer, 'where they ate thur turnips raw.'

This time the engine was facing the right way round.

Within an hour they were back in the barracks.

Two weeks later the lino arrived. Two men carried it into the kitchen and stood it up against the wall beside the dresser. It was thick as a telegraph pole and tied round the middle with binder twine.

Next morning, as she combed his hair, his mother promised he could help her lay it.

His father was over by the window shaving.

The lino, steadied by its own weight, sloped from wall to floor.

In the jut of the window stood an old sink holding a basin of water. Nailed to the window frame was a razor-strop and propped by the catch a mirror. His father had his back to them. Like a harness, his braces dangled round his rump. Crouching before his image he flapped the cut-throat across his cheek. The razor shone like a silver wing above a field of snow.

Suddenly the roll of lino began to move. His father couldn't see it coming towards him. The boy and his mother, transfixed, couldn't stop it. Gathering momentum as it slipped along the damp wall it came to the window recess where it fell free and with considerable force thwacked into the back of his father's head.

His legs buckled.

His mother's scream died as the lino hit the floor. She always panicked.

'Daddy, Daddy, are you all right?'

Stunned, eyes staring into the mirror, he stood in rigid calm, the cut-throat still as a hawk above his face.

In the frozen silence his mother rolled the lino in against the wall.

'That's what should have been done with it when they delivered it,' said his father.

Shaking his head he jabbed the blade along his upper lip.

The sound of the lino hitting his father's skull had burst into the boy's mind in an explosion of blood

70

and snapping elastic. The pulpy thwack was a flash of sound. Sounds were pictures too.

He was frightened. His father smiled at him and winked.

'Some head, hah?'

'Why did it move like that, Daddy?'

'Why wouldn't it and us going around the sun?'

Before things outside his control he barely flinched. He could cope with sickness, bad news, sudden blows, going round the sun. Sawing timber, however, mending the hen-house, getting his arms into his greatcoat, cobbling on wet days – all operations within his power – drove him mad.

'What's lino made from?'

'I don't know.'

'Canvas and linseed. Now you know. And knowledge doesn't weigh you down. But it's still a mystery how words get on our tongues.'

Against the towel draped over his wrist he cleaned the razor with careful sideways movements. Flipping the basin over, the water choked and gurgled out the sink.

Buttoning his uniform he left the married quarters for the barracks's day room.

The boy stole after him and glimpsed him through the window, sitting at the office table, pen poised in his hand, calm, rigid and staring into space.

When it was down, the lino made the old furniture shabby and unreal. Its shiny newness crinkled under foot like eggshell.

His mother was pleased with it and so was his father.

During the Rosary that evening he saw them admiring it and when his father got up off his knees he said it was worth the money.

He kissed them both. His father's cheek smelled of carbolic soap and cooking apples.

'Good boy, goodnight now.'

In the flaking darkness the crown of thorns above the bed began to dance and the shadowy man towered above the wardrobe.

He covered his head with the bed clothes but there in the blackness twisted the hanged man, staring at him with bulging eyes. He tried thinking of rice pudding, trains and whin bushes burning on the hills along the Border. But the wardrobe door creaked open and there was the button-eyed fox, smelling of moth-balls and alert for killer dogs. Lost in the hidden night he was awoken by screams.

His mother was standing by the bed, the oil lamp in her hand. Her hysterical shrieks and high-pitched suffocating sobs clawed at his ears and terrified his heart. Even whilst she was dragging him out on to the floor he thought it was a dream. Her hair hung loose about her shoulders and her eyes rolled in dancing madness. The flame of the lamp burned black against the globe.

'Help, help. Quick, quick.'

She ran to the door but afraid to open it came back and grabbed him by the hand. She seemed to the boy to be running round in painful circles like a bird with a broken wing. He began to cry. He still hoped it was all a nightmare but somehow knew it wasn't when he saw the familiar mole on her neck with the single black hair growing from it.

He didn't know what to do. More to check on reality than for refuge he clung to her and buried his head in her belly. He definitely wasn't dreaming. This was his mother, this was him and they were for some reason standing crying in the middle of the frightening night.

'Mammy, Mammy, Mammy, what's happening?'

She clutched him in a frozen embrace. 'Daddy's dying, Daddy's dying, Daddy's dying.'

In the stillness of the words swooning down on his heart he heard groans coming from his father's room.

When they went in to him he was lying on his side, his eyes wide open. His mother reached to touch him but drew her hand back. He wasn't aware of their presence. He stared, glassy-eyed, at his own reflection which stared back at him from the full-length mirror in the corner of the room. Round his mouth was white froth. His moans were deep and seemed to have no connection with his body. His mother began saying an act of contrition in his ear but couldn't continue. She ran out of the room.

The boy looked from his father in the bed to his father in the mirror. The blankets were gripped up to his chin so only his head was visible. His face was pale as candle, the eyes glistening like frost. He thought of the rabbits lying dead on the floor of the railway carriage. Four eyes there. Two eyes in the bed. Two eyes in the mirror. Two eyes hanging down in the wardrobe. Ten eyes.

He stroked his father's forehead. It was cold, stiff.

Unwrapping the rosary from the bed-head he opened the crucifix and held to his lips the part with the bit of wood that had touched a bit of wood from the cross that Jesus died on.

His father gurgled, moaned and gave out a convulsed roar that lifted the boy with fear and threw him down quaking with terror against the bedroom door.

It was blood-curdling and grotesque, like a fun-fair Hall of Mirrors and Haunted House combined.

'Oh, Holy God, please let this be a nightmare only.' The words rang round the cold walls mocking his fear. It was no nightmare. That was his father, now moaning quietly, staring in imbecilic blankness at his own image, the eyes wide open but powerless to command.

His mother came back in and searched his father's trouser pockets until she found a bunch of keys. In a whirl of words she told him she was going round to the day room to phone for the doctor and the priest. She took the oil lamp with her.

Every strangled howl that came from the bed heaped up the black night blacker, so that the boy felt he was drowning in a room of tar. He was stuck in shivering fright. Unable to stop it he felt the urine gush into his pyjamas, run hotly down his leg and over his freezing feet.

His father called it pooley. So there was a pool of pooley on the bedside mat. Normally he wasn't even allowed into his father's room and yet here he was widdling on the floor and his father only a few feet away in the bed! It was mad. It was Hell.

He felt desperately ashamed. How was he going to hide it from his mother? And when the priest came and the doctor, they couldn't fail to notice! They'd actually be standing in it attending his father!

On the other side of the wall he could hear his mother winding the handle of the telephone and shouting gibberish to the operator. She took ages to explain that her husband was dying and she wanted to be put through to Dr Langan in Cavan town.

The boy stumbled to the window and drew back the curtains. The moon was torn, the clouds tattered by the wind.

He got on his knees and fumbled under the bed for the chamber pot he knew was there. Finding it he upended it on the mat and pushed the lot under the bed. He hoped when his mother discovered it she would think it had been accidentally kicked over.

In the creeping moonlight his father looked like a big, horrible, vomiting baby. At least if he died the horrible groaning would stop. Compared to this, the picture of Jesus over his bed, the shadowy man by the wardrobe, the hanged man, they were just ice cream and lollipops. Feeling guilty he knelt to pray for his father but only on one knee so he'd be ready to bolt if he came anywhere near him.

Down in the hen-house the rooster began to crow. He didn't like the noises his father was making either. It was as if he had a bone stuck in his brain and was trying to vomit it out.

Uncomfortable in his wet pyjamas he took the bottom

part off and was about to go and get his pants when his mother came back. She was too distracted to notice him flinging the pyjamas under the bed.

She ordered him to run up to Guard Hegarty and tell him to come quick, his father was dying.

Though he was glad to be away from the hell-hole of the groaning room now he found himself in the middle of the road, completely naked except for his pyjama jacket. He felt foolish but at least it was dark. He ran towards Hegarty's house, half a mile away.

He wondered if the man in the moon could see down as far as his bare bum.

Inside the desmesne wall the wind whipped through the trees and the watery moon shone on the roadway filling the potholes to the brim.

Every scurrying leaf he took to be a rat and the bellows breathing of cattle on the other side of the hedge terrified him. A pheasant rose up and in a splutter of honks crashed up into the night.

The night made every familiar tree and bush utterly foreign. He felt lost in a far-off country.

At last Hegarty answered the door.

'Come quick, Daddy's dying.'

He had a candle in his hand and peered down at the boy trying to make him out. Still half asleep he couldn't quite believe his ears.

'Mammy told me to get you quick.'

'God bless us, dying?'

He shouted in to his wife, banged the door after him and ran off down the road towards the barracks.

Hegarty had thick grey hair, wore glasses and was within two years of retiring. His wife was twenty-five years younger than him.

The boy ran behind him and was glad Hegarty looked so funny trying to run in unlaced boots and holding up his trousers with one hand. He was out of breath and coughing. He smoked packets of Afton Major every day and drank his fill in Reilly's pub most evenings.

A motor car came behind them, the headlights shafting a tunnel through the black.

'This'll be the priest,' said Hegarty, 'keep in. He's a holy terror behind a wheel.'

The boy covered his bum with his hands and hoped the priest wouldn't notice.

The car sped past and as the lights swept the desmesne gates they saw the dazzled surprise on ex-Private Jimmy Kelly's face as he came riding out, the handlebars of his bicycle laden with dead rabbits.

'It's home in your bed you should be,' shouted Hegarty, 'instead of out poaching, you blaggard.'

'Begod if I had your wife that's where I would be! Instead of gandering about in the small hours like a blind horse. What the hell's goin' on anyway?'

'None of your business.'

The rabbits hung limp, their eyes dancing dead like his father's in the mirror.

When they reached the barracks and went into the room the priest was praying into his father's ear, pausing, giving each word a chance to sink home. When not speaking, his lower lip trembled continuously, a habit which gave his face a cranky appearance.

His father was still groaning, his lips covered with thick frothy gobs.

The boy went into his mother's room and put on his pants. From under the crown of thorns Jesus winked at him.

'I'm not so frightening after all, am I?'

'No, Jesus, you're not.'

When he came out again the doctor had arrived and his mother had calmed down.

Priest, doctor, Guard Hegarty and his mother stood looking in silence at his father. Hegarty burped and the priest looked at him with trembling lip.

Suddenly the groans began to die away, then stop. His father moved in the bed, shut his eyes, opened them again and stared straight at the boy. Lifting himself up in the bed he was amazed to see the room full of people.

'You're all right, Sergeant,' said Dr Langan. 'You've had a bad turn but you're over the worst of it now.'

His father groped for his pocket watch, looped over the bed-head. The gold lid flicked open and he stared at the hands.

With the back of his hand he wiped his mouth. He looked pale, shocked and ashamed.

His mother's eyes were red and swollen from crying. Her hair hung like a hank of flax on one side of her head with a few stray wisps sticking straight out on the other side. She looked as if her nerves had snapped.

His father was looking at his mother with a puzzled, lost expression. He was appealing silently to her for help and explanation. Like a child.

'It was the lino hitting your head, that's what did it.'

'Oh that's what did it,' said the priest.

'Certainly,' said Dr Langan, 'that appears at the moment to be the most likely explanation. Without a doubt.'

'I've got a splitting headache, that's one sure thing, anyway,' said his father.

'God help us tonight,' said his mother, catching a glimpse of herself in the mirror.

The boy, catching a glimpse of his pyjama bottoms under the bed, sunk to his knees. He would have to get them. If his mother discovered them there she would guess what had happened.

'That's a good boy,' said the priest.

But though his head was bowed and he had one hand on his forehead, he wasn't praying. His other hand was groping for the pyjamas. When he felt them he pulled them towards him and, hidden by the end of the bed, fumbled them up his trouser leg.

His left leg bulging unnaturally he left the room.

He lay in bed listening to the dull voices and waiting for his mother to come to him. When she did he butted his head into her breast wanting to be warm and to forget.

'Don't.'

'Was it a nightmare, Mammy?'

'Yes. A real one.'

*

The nightmare recurred. Always in the heart of night and always they awoke a few seconds before each attack. It was uncanny. They lay rigid, waiting for the long drawn-out howl of desperate entrapment. It cut them with knifing fear. But they didn't go into his room.

The doctor told his mother that the fit had struck, having lain dormant in his brain since childhood. He warned against alcohol and prescribed one phenobarbitone pill per day.

Since he was unaware of them they never told his father when he had an attack. 'What he doesn't know won't trouble him,' the doctor said to his mother.

They were protecting him from himself and from the village gossips. If it became known that the Sergeant had fits his job could be at risk.

The secret was a burden to them. And when some mornings his father complained of a headache the boy had to look away from his eyes, hating the secret because it kept his heart distant from his father.

He wanted to tell him why he had to take the pill. Half the reason his father hated it was he didn't know why he had to swallow it down.

Most days he tried to escape the little white eye of pill. Wet cobbling days were the worst.

The boy looked at the pill. It was there on the blue lino, just by the leg of the table.

His father belted the bare anvil with the hammer. He stopped, stared out at the pouring rain and then at the boy.

He picked the little white eye from the lino and handed it to his father.

He took it and with a bitter grimace swallowed it down.

His mother smiled to him. There would be no attack tonight.

MOTH

E<small>ACH EVENING HE LIT</small> the tilley lamp. His father
said it was a privilege, not a duty.

'He's some man can turn dark to light.'

'Am I a man, Daddy?'

'Not the way you're pumping that, you're not. Steady,
steady. Mantles cost money, you know.'

A new mantle fresh from its cellophane packet felt
shiny, lacey. Like his mother's fancy bloomers. But flame
transformed it. Under pressure, oil rose up the stem and
out the nozzle in a fine drizzle. Warmed by burning pads
of methylated spirit it turned to vapour. This vapour
mixed with air and puffed the mantle to a flakey ball of
golden light. It was magic.

But once fired the mantle was extremely delicate. A
nudge, draught or insect could destroy it.

He raised the lamp and gently hung it on its nail up
the wall. Framed in the shadows above was his father's
rifle, still and silent as a painting. A moth zigged up and
landed on the butt.

The boy watched it and listened to the tilley dishing out golden light with a creamy sigh.

'What's a mantle made out of?'

'I haven't a clue, Daddy.'

'No and you never will if you never ask.'

Peering out at the pitchy night he drew the curtains. There wasn't a speck of light in the sky or in the scattering of houses along the hills.

He sat and with the burnt end of a matchstick scraped dirt and crumbs from the crevice running along the table top.

Every evening his mother worked the sewing machine, her fingers feeding cloth to the needle, her swollen legs operating the treadle. His father gone out, he liked being alone with her. There was no fear in him watching her work. Her concentration was total but gentle. Unlike his father who was all scraggy rage and awkwardness.

She wore dark-grey stockings to hide the elastic bandages. Blood gushed thickly in her swollen veins and had to be held in. Like wrapping burst pipes with bicycle tubes.

'Let me do it.'

He went to her and stuck his foot in on the treadle. The wheel whirred and his mother fed the hem of a blue dress to the needle, her wedding ring glinting in the light.

Bending his face to her neck, he smelt her skin. It was warm, powdery and mantle soft.

'Where do we go when we're dead?'

'No one knows. But don't say I said so.'

A moth landed on the curtains. Wings widespread it

84

stumbled into a fold. Only its head reappeared and its long tongue, which kept curving in and out. The tongue was the colour of a stick of barley sugar and the head reminded the boy of an owl.

His mother put both feet on the treadle, the belted wheel speeding to a blur, the connector rod dancing up and down like a demented gymnast on a high bar.

Her nightly task was removing the bandages and rolling them tightly for the morning.

Uncoiled they lay on the floor by her bare feet. Only her toes were free of veins. They were pale as suet but elsewhere the skin bulged knotty blue.

Sometimes his father challenged her to a race. They'd each roll up a bandage, the boy judging who finished first.

It was a game. His father's last attempt to rescue something from the day.

Bandages snaking up from the floor to their fingers, they sat poised, waiting for the boy to shout 'Go', his mother laughing, his father looking shyly into her hurt eyes.

His mother always won. Reeling in the cloth her fingers spun like bobbins and when she had finished her roll was wad-tight.

His father's clumsy fingers were no match for her. This was part of the fun. It was the one occasion he tolerated his own clumsiness. The contest was of no importance to him, and his thumby attempts to roll the bandage neatly made them laugh. Laughter softened his mother. In happiness as in sorrow she cried easily. Wet pearls spurted from her eyes and sometimes when his father snatched the bandage from her hands, so that she had to start all over again, she slipped from the chair to the floor in helpless hysterics.

'It's not fair, it's not fair. I'll die laughing.'

'Not a bad way to go, let me tell you.'

Wild joy danced out of his father's eyes.

'I've won, I've won.'

'No you haven't. Mammy won. You cheated. Anyway, yours is more like a scraw than a roll.'

'Ah-hah, you magpie, there'll be white crows the day you're on my side.'

'A magpie is half a white crow. So I must be half on your side anyway.'

'Oh we're very quick, aren't we? You're so quick you could catch a fart and rub grease into it.'

Behind their laughter was hidden meaning. When his mother looked into his father's eyes, the boy, embarrassed and not knowing why, stared at the floor.

The game over he watched him looking at her as she leaned in over the range with a saucepan of milk.

Heated, she served it to his father in a pint glass.

'Grand.'

The two rolls of bandages were placed on top of the radio. Puttees, his father called them.

'What's a puttee?'

'You've told me before. A band of cloth twisted from the ankle to the knee, worn to support the leg. Am I right, Daddy?'

'Yes and you're half left.'

He was always testing the boy, fearful he was a dunce.

'No knowledge – no money. No money – poverty all your live long days.'

'What about the Franciscans – they're poor, Daddy? But they've got brains.'

'Off to bed outa that and don't be annoying us. Go on now.'

He kissed the stubbled jaw. It was warm and hard, like a stone in the sun.

'Goodnight. You're a great boy.'

He loved his father's praise. Craved it. And hated that weakness in himself.

'Look, Daddy, look how high I can kick the ball.'

'Yes and look at the state of your shoes.'

A clip of the tongue always brought him back to earth. He was a kite, and his father's words string tugging him down.

'Don't be too hard on the boy.'

'Yes and don't you be too soft on him.'

He was middle ground with the lie of the land all his mother's way. It wasn't fair on his father. Why couldn't love be equal in every direction?

His father came in one night and looked at him as he lay in bed. He stood in the middle of the room holding an oil lamp. His tunic hung open, the silver whistle chain dangling free and the long black whangs of his boots undone.

'Very soon you'll have to sleep on your own. We'll fix up a bed for you in the spare room.'

The thought of sleeping away from his mother's warmth turned him cold with fear and anger.

'Why?'

'That's why.'

Gripping the lamp steady so that the flame burnt straight up the globe, his father looked down at him. Wick eyes blazing full.

'You don't know you're alive.'

'I do.'

'What? What are you talking about?'

'I feel myself here and I can see you standing there.'

'No, you jackass you! What I mean is you don't know how lucky you are.'

The buttonhole hook of the silver chain hung down his tunic like an upended question mark.

He gripped the blankets to his chin and wished his father would leave. But he stayed in the room, jingling coins in his pocket, staring at his dark reflection in the washstand mirror. Then he began talking about his own father.

'Black Jack. He was known as that. They went to Warrington in Lancashire every year for the harvest. Going over on the boat the men were drinking. A fight broke out. Dada cleared the deck. Captain, sailors, men. They couldn't hold him. His fists were rocks. Your uncle Pat and me – many's the clout he gave us. Crack. When he hit you, you stayed hit for days.'

The lamp tilting, flame hit the globe and began smoking. A dark patch spread up the glass.

'Why did he hit you, Daddy?'

'For reasons best known to himself. Or if you botched work. Crack.'

A small white moth flittered the room.

He knew if his father ever hit him, he'd stay hit for centuries.

In the amber silence the flame tongued the globe. The boy knew it was going to crack. He could smell the dull oily vapour. He was frightened of his father's lost mood.

'Dream of the dead and it brings luck.'

The tiny moth whirled the lamp, then landed on it.

With a tinkling sound a crack, sharp as pain and clean as an icicle, ran up the globe from the butt to the rim.

His father jolted from his thoughts and looked at the lamp.

'Oh cripes.'

Banging out he shuffled across the hallway and into his own room. The boy heard his boots hit the floor and the springs of the iron bed squealing. Then his angry shout in the dark – 'What the hell's keeping her?'

His mother was visiting neighbours. His father hated her being out. So did the boy.

The house without her was an empty grate. Desperate for her return, unable to sleep, he lay, eyes open, listening to the scuttering mice scratching across the ceiling. Mice were climbers. One morning he watched one climbing up the pebble-dashed wall of the barracks, sniffing, twisting, swishing but all the time its delicate paws calmly feeling from pebble to pebble until at last it disappeared through a crack in the weatherboard.

'How did he know the crack was there?' said his father, 'that's what I'd like to know. Thank God Mr Rat prefers the ground.'

He didn't like mice, he certainly didn't like rats and ever since that night his father stared down at him, threatening banishment from his mother's bed, he hated moths.

So far, though, he hadn't been evicted. And tonight he was alone with her.

As she sewed at the machine he sat close to her, imagining the needle and her fingers a giant cloth-devouring spider. Glancing up he saw the big moth still peeping down at him from the folds of the curtain.

'Mammy, are moths magic?'

'Not that I know of. Why?'

'They can crack lamps.'

'Can they? They love light, that I do know. They commit suicide for it.'

'I always want to sleep in your bed. Not in the spare room. I'm not moving, I'm not. Why do I have to?'

His mother, surprised at his outburst, looked at him and laughed gently. Then the door opened and his father stepped in.

He'd been away all day at a football match and was in mufti – a white mackintosh over a tweed jacket, open-necked blue shirt, grey trousers and shoes.

He stood leaning against the wall, his handsome face twisted in a silly drunken grin.

A moustache of porter stained his upper lip.

'Your tea's on the table.' His mother hated drink.

His father lurched to the table and sat without removing his coat and cap.

'Guess who I met in Cavan?'

'I couldn't care less.'

His father laughed – too loudly for the reality of the moment.

'An admirer of yours.'

Sticking his fork into a tomato, slowly raising it towards his mouth, lowering his head, he bit into it.

A squirt of juice and seed splattered up the wall.

His mother sighed and sucked her tongue against the roof of her mouth in annoyance.

'Come on, guess. You know him.'

'Dr Langan.' She spat a piece of thread from her lips.

In a pretence of annoyance, his father threw down his fork.

'How the hell did you know?'

'Who else could it be?'

'"By the Lord Harry, Sergeant," says he, "she's an exquisite woman."'

'Did he indeed? The old fool.'

She was pleased. The boy could see it in her eyes. She loved doctors and priests. 'Body and soul merchants', his father called them.

'He says I ought to move you into the town. Says you're lost out here in Butlershill.'

Moistening a thread end, she fed it to the needle eye and started sewing again.

His father, stony still in silence, hunched over his

plate, staring at a piece of ham dangling on the end of his knife.

A scrape of mustard daubed the plate. Beetroot bled over the lettuce. The colours on a pigeon's chest.

His mother began to hum a tune. Her family had been well-to-do merchants. Until drink ruined them, they had a grocery and hardware shop and the only bakery in the West of Ireland. She had been educated by French nuns in a boarding school in Mayo.

Whenever she was annoyed she hummed the 'Marseillaise'.

His father looked over at her. He was tone deaf but this never prevented him singing, especially when he was drunk. He had two songs – 'Pasadena' and 'Greensleeves'.

'In Pasadena where grass is green now . . .'

'Greensleeves you are my delight . . .'

In his mouth both songs sounded the same.

He sang to the ham dangling on his fork. His mother hummed to the hem of her dress.

The boy laughed. They looked at him. To see whose side he was on. His father's look was the most honest. There was no trace of emotional blackmail in it. He rarely showed his feelings.

But if love couldn't be shown, how did you know it was there? You hoped.

Sewing finished, his mother allowed him to return the machine to its belly, letting the flap down with a slap.

'You'd get better music from a corncrake!' said his mother.

'I'll admit it, none of us could sing. The braying ass made us jealous.'

'If you can talk, you should be able to sing. That's what the nuns always said.'

'I suppose if you can walk, you should be able to jump like a flea?'

With the back of his fingers he flicked the plate of food away and hands on the edge pushed himself from the table.

The chair legs screeched and waddled over the lino.

'Hang me cap.'

Reaching for the peak the boy could smell the porter. The cap was damp from rain on the outside and sweat on the inside.

'What's mufti?'

'Leave the boy alone.'

'I'm not talking to you.'

'No, you're talking at me.'

'If you're so clever, what are you doing here?'

His mother gathered up her scissors, spools, pins and put them back into the red cake tin with the rest of her sewing materials.

The boy knew she had no answer to the question. When her father signed away the family business her only salvation was marriage. Or England.

His father moved to the range and stood with his back to them, looking at the picture of the Sacred Heart.

His mother put the sewing box on top of the dresser. Her neck in the light was golden, the mole on it a crumb of flesh.

His father spat on the range, the sud frazzling to a brown stain.

'In Pasadena where grass is green now . . .'

He turned, faced them, a grin on one corner of his mouth.

'Love at first sight. With your mother. I never asked how much she had. Uncle Alec introduced us. I was a detective with him in Dublin Castle in those days. I said, "Will you?" and she said, "Yes." That was that and this is now. I'll tell you this, me buck, if you ever get anyone half as good as your mother, you'll be the luckiest man in Ireland.'

His eyes misted. Like ice forming on window panes. He was trying to cry, to show he cared, to show he loved them.

He stood stiffly, feet apart, head high, shoulders back, pretending to be sober. The mackintosh hung down to his ankles and rustled like canvas every time he jerked his body.

'Yes. Love at first sight. When I think of it. Ah, when I think of it. No veins in those legs then.'

The boy's mother sat staring at the moth moving along the curtain, going in and out of the folds.

His father went to her and gripped her shoulders. She looked up at him. He lifted her, twisted his arms round her, pressed her to his body, hid her in the folds of his coat.

The boy watched their shut eyes.

Reaching out, his father pulled him in between them, where pressed by their bodies he was hidden from the night and the moth swirling about their heads.

The force of their bodies took his breath away and when he felt his father's flesh press into his back he squirmed free.

The donkey on the hill behind the barracks; his flesh hung down on hot days, flies buzzing it.

His father went back to the range and taking off his mackintosh threw it into the armchair. On the inside of the coat was a strip of bicycle tube, patched over a rip. The tube puckered from the surface but like all his father's handiwork somehow held.

'You can go to bed now and sleep it off.'

'Sleep what off?'

His mood changed, his face looked long and hard as a milestone. He began hitting the palm of his left hand with his right fist.

The boy could see the fear flooding into his mother. She removed her apron and sat folding it on her lap. Taking off her spectacles, she flipped the legs inwards, wrapped them in the apron and put them away in a drawer of the sewing machine.

'Sleep what off?' He staggered forward, burping. 'I've always paid my way. I don't owe any man one penny. Not one red cent. You had no money. And I didn't ask you for any. Every single damn thing I have, I got meself. No one helped me or gave me a damn thing I didn't earn the hard way. Is that true or isn't it?'

His face was a dung-fork of thistles, his skin grey from tension, cheekbones high and sharp, teeth in a grind of temper.

'Take it easy, you're frightening the boy.'

In this mood his father was a mad horse. Petrified, he went to the door and put his hand on the knob, ready to bolt.

'Where do you think you're going?'

'I think I'm going out, Daddy.'

'Is there something the matter with your brain? I think I see you standing there.'

For a moment his father's play on meaning escaped him. He looked to his mother for help.

She was wearing her practised smile of martyrdom, which made her more beautiful and innocent than ever and which enraged his father even more.

'Yes, sit there like a weeping saint. "Oh don't touch me, I'm the Blessed Virgin's best friend!" What am I supposed to do – sleep on my own for the rest of me days, like a convict?'

So that was it. Something to do with that flesh of men and women. Flesh hung down or stood up and imprisoned all humans, birds and beasts. Or set them free.

The clock on the mantelpiece tocked. The tilley lamp sighed. The world shrank to a cheap and tawdry cell.

Half the dresser crockery was cracked, the dresser itself bored along the bottom with woodworm. The door of the bookcase hung from the top hinge only and the chairs were an odd collection from the various stations in which his father had served.

Over by the sink, silver fish swam the damp walls and a wood-louse crawling the skirting board fell to the floor, where it lay arching and wriggling, trying to right itself.

The world seemed trapped in his father's rage.

'If any man gets in my road tonight . . . or the Super comes out from Cavan, snooping . . . I'll, I'll . . .'

His tongue thick with anger, the words came out gungy.

Turning from them, he gripped either end of the mantelpiece and stood looking at the Sacred Heart. The boy moved to the door again. Whipping round, his father stepped forward and exploded his fist into the back of the old leather armchair. The chair went flying backwards, his father tumbling after it, and when he withdrew his fist, horse-hair guts and a spring burst out with his bleeding fingers. Blood blobbed the lino. His mother stood to help.

'I don't want anything from you, I don't want anything at all!'

Sick at the irony of his own words, he slumped vomiting across the table, pounding a plate to pieces with his hand.

The boy clung to his mother, crying and squealing like a terrified dog.

A wipe of sick smearing his face, his father grabbed his tunic from the back of the door and went down to his room.

'Hush now, hush, it's all over now.'

Later they heard him going out, slamming the door so hard the tilley lamp jumped on its nail.

The lettuce and the beetroot swam in the brown sick. It looked like gravy. It was so sour the smell ripped the nose and the back of the throat.

They cleaned it, his mother offering it up as a prayer to God for forgiveness.

'What's a sin, Mammy?'

'No one knows. But don't say I said so. Wasted food – that's a sin.'

Side by side they sat at the range, leaning in over it, elbows resting on it, feeling the dying heat. To save fuel, each evening after tea the fire was allowed to burn down.

In the chimney the wind grunted, and out over the desmesne crows clacked and tattered at the black night.

He looked over at the wood-louse. It was still struggling to right itself.

From the open drain at the rear of the barracks came the snap of steel teeth and the agonised squeals of a rat.

He plugged his ears, sang loudly, thought of jelly and ice cream but couldn't block the rat from his mind.

His father set the trap, baiting it with bacon rinds.

It never failed. Each morning there was either a dead rat or a rat still alive, caught by its leg, the skin pulled away from the flesh in its attempts to break free.

'It's cruel, Daddy.'

'Sure the beggars would eat us out of house and home if we didn't do something. Mr Rat is some boyo, let me tell you.'

He hated the way he made the rat into a person. That made it even worse. He hated looking at the raw, purple flesh, the fur peeled down to the claw, hated the fresh blood on the bait plate, hated the sharp crack as his father finished them off with a spade.

Unplugging his ears, he went to the wood-louse and, not knowing why, crushed it underfoot.

The moth brushed his face, zigged the room, then settled on the lampshade.

'Go down to the village and get the milk like a good boy.'

He ran out of the barracks, glad to escape.

As soon as he went out the gate, however, he gasped for breath as if drowning. Massive clouds wrapped the earth. He couldn't see the hills, the trees, the road beneath him. He could feel the silvery milk can in his hand but couldn't see it. The road to the village was a black river and he was trying to wade through it, way out of his depth.

There wasn't a trace of the moon or a single star. The world was waxy black, oceans deep and heavy. The night weighed down like the police greatcoats they used on the bed as extra blankets.

He heard footsteps approaching and recognised the staggering hobnailed boots of the drunken postman.

He was as usual, though alone, heaping curses on his wife.

'If she was afire I wouldn't piss on her.'

Sensing the boy's presence he stopped and called out.

'Man or baste, hah?'

The boy was glad he had come along.

'If I was a beast, you couldn't have expected an answer, Charlie.'

'What's that, you scut you?'

'It's, it's very dark, isn't it, Charlie?'

'Go way, you mouse you, you're all right. Your father's down there clearing the pubs.'

Filled with forebodings at the thought of his father clearing the pubs and he drunk himself, he walked on, guiding himself by touching the long grass and dock edging the road.

In the distance at the bottom of the hill a slice of light cut through the dark. It was coming from the gable window in the Methodist chapel. It flowed across the road like a golden stream between two high banks of black.

He could hear the congregation singing a hymn, the words flickering out into the night, brave as candle flame.

Hurrying down the hill, he reached the light and jumped from the darkness into it, then out again the other side. Stretching his arm out, he separated it from the rest of his body on the sharp edge of light and dark.

Going through the gate he went into the chapel porch and peeped in the door.

The chapel was small, bare, cold and scrubbed. And so was the congregation.

The men wore dark suits, the women prim frocks. There was no altar or crucifixes and no one seemed in charge. They stood clasping Bibles and singing.

> All things bright and beautiful
> All creatures great and small . . .

On a wall was a handwritten notice – 'The wages of sin is DEATH.'

His father was right. There wasn't a fat face or body amongst them.

'They're thin from work and making money. That's their religion. And looking at pictures of the English Queen in the *Irish Times*.'

'They're doing you no harm anyway,' said his mother.

He came back out on the path. By the gate was a stack of bicycles and parked along the road a few cars.

When he came into the village, light from the few shops and houses splashed the street, lying on the dark like wipes of butter on burnt toast.

On the village green a goat bleeted angrily. It was always there, tethered and crying.

Because it was Sunday, Tully's pub and shop were closed. He went to the adjoining house and knocked on the open door.

Across the green he could see two men slipping into Reilly's pub, the door closing quickly, the bolt shot home with a dull clank. The village was a triangle of buildings with the green in the middle. Three roads led out of it. One to Fermanagh, one to Monaghan, one to Cavan town.

When they first arrived in it, his mother counted the shops and houses.

'Fourteen. Like the stations of the Cross,' she sobbed.

'Come on now,' said his father, 'we'll get used to it.'

He knocked again at Tully's door. Now he could hear voices within. The grunts of drunkards, raised in agreement, and the voice of Tully himself, shrilling in anger. Then silence.

A blast of wind lifted the loose corrugated sheet on the roof of the Customs hut.

A ragged tear appearing in the clouds, he glimpsed the leper moon and, in the watery light falling on the trees, could see the wind-whipped leaves, swishing and twisting like shoals of netted fish.

'Clear outa hell home now, or I'll summons every man Jack of you!'

His father's voice. From inside Tully's, clearing it. Pubs were shut on Sundays but drinking took place in back parlours, behind drawn blinds. There was a rush to the door of men escaping before their names were taken. The boy recognised them – farmers, labourers, the carpenter, his friend the bicycle mechanic and 'The Boxer' Duffy, who lived across the Border.

From the shadows, the boy watched his father connect with a kick to the carpenter's rear, pitching the man comically on to his hands and knees.

The raised boot hung vast on the street. The welt, inches thick from an accumulation of repairs to the sole, made his foot appear even larger than it was already.

The Boxer Duffy, ex-clerical student, ex-boxer, brought low by drink, crouched in a fighting posture, his fists just visible in the pool of door light.

'I don't live in your jurisdiction, so you can do your worst, Sergeant. I've bate better men with the flat of me cap.'

His father drew his truncheon.

'Away, you reprobate, before I mangle you!'

Backing off, The Boxer Duffy fell over the carpenter,

who was still drunkenly trying to raise himself from the ground.

'All right, Sergeant, all right,' shouted the carpenter, 'I'm going, I'm going. When I can get me arse to come with me. You might as well be kicked by a mad horse.'

The light shining round him, his father stood in the doorway, like a rock on fire, watching the men depart.

He turned to face Tully, whose normally red face was pale with fury. Tully with land straddling the Border and owning pub, shop and hearse had a financial hold on most of the people in the district.

'You can't come in here throwing your weight around. You never touch Reilly's over there, do you? No, because you rely on him for lifts to football matches. And you and your cronies drink there, after hours, whenever you want to. It's ojus what the rest of us have to put up with and I'm telling you, Sergeant, I'm not standing for it a day longer.'

A malicious grin twisted his father's lips as he swayed in the doorway, truculent and superior. Tully was squealing and that was the way he liked it.

'I'll have your licence one of these fine days, me buck. I caught those men red-handed. Not content with all your loot, you have to milk the last rex from the poor fools, who should on a Sunday be home saying their prayers, instead of getting rooked by you, with your watered-down hooch and sour porter. Go way, man, before I lug you up to the cell.'

Loot. Rex. Rooked. Hooch. Lug. Words were bullets.

The thin red moustache on Tully's lip wriggled.

'I'm reporting you to Dublin,' he screamed, standing on his tiptoes for emphasis.

He was a small wiry man, quick as a ferret. The boy often watched him going about the village, humming to himself. The same three notes constantly repeated.

A confirmed bachelor, he neither smoked nor drank and boasted he needed less than six hours' sleep a night.

'Six hours for a man. Seven for a woman. Eight for a pig.'

It was said he had £80,000 in the bank in Cavan.

His father hated him.

'You can report me to Timbuktu for all the good it'll do you. Headquarters know your form. They have a file on you going back years.'

This was quite possibly true. The man was a known smuggler who somehow always managed to escape pursuing Customs men.

His father still had his truncheon in his hand. Tully looked at him and could see his dangerous mood.

Standing in the shadows the boy could see it too. Could sense him deliberately stoking up his frustrations to explosion point.

Tully walked away, then came back.

'Sergeant, Sergeant, we all have to live here. You've got your duty to do but we all have to make a living. Those men were having a well-earned drink. They drove cattle for me all day yesterday. No money changed hands. The drinks were on the house.'

He smiled up at his father. The smile revealed his upper gum and row of tiny teeth.

His father wanted blood.

'You stick to the law or I'll see to it the law sticks to you, me buck.'

He tapped home each word on the door-jamb with his truncheon.

Tully froze. He could take no more. His words when they came were calm, dry and deadly.

'Right. You asked for it, Sergeant. I'm going to fix you once and for all.'

He ran from the hallway and a few seconds later the boy could see candle-light quivering the shut darkness of the shop.

Taking a torch from his pocket, his father turned and flashed it, the beam hitting the boy right between the eyes, trapping him like a stunned rabbit.

But before he could say anything Tully was back in the hallway, dancing about on his toes, waving a red notebook.

The boy recognised it as his mother's grocery book. Each item ordered was entered, added up and paid for at the end of the month. The boy knew his mother was having difficulty making ends meet. Tully, ranting at his father, thumbed the book from page to page. His shouts were so high-pitched they seemed to be piping out the top of his head.

'You see that? You see that? Don't think you can come in here throwing your weight around. See? See?'

The significance of his words and the figures in red ink escaped his father,

'Are you blind? Started off there. £10. £20. Carried

over. £50 there. Carried over to the following month. And the following. July, £80. Ever since you came here. See? See?'

Staring dumbly at him, his father swallowed hard, his Adam's apple popping in his long neck.

'What are you talking about, man?'

'Your wife owes me £200, Sergeant, that's what I'm talking about. £200. So don't come in here again until you pay up or it's me that'll stick the law on you, me buck!'

He shut the book with a slap against his thigh.

A daddy-long-legs flew in from the street and landed on Tully's rolled-up shirt sleeve.

'Show me.' In a wild hope he was bluffing, his father snatched the notebook from Tully's hand.

The boy crept up to the door and when his father opened the last page, he could plainly see the fatal words – 'Outstanding Amount To Date – £200.'

The words were in blue ink, the sum in red and underlined twice.

His father was cornered. His chest began to heave and a groan rattled in his throat.

The boy could see that Tully was already regretting his action. If his father had the money, the debt would be paid but the account taken across the street to Reilly's,

Leaning against the door, his head and eyes screwed up in agony, his tongue hooked out on his bottom lip, his father let out a long howl of desperate rage that sent a flock of crows in the demesne screeching into the sky and brought a face to every window in the village.

The boy's legs went rubbery and the milk can clattered from his hand.

Now his father was bending double, clutching at his stomach.

'I'm going to murder her.'

The boy turned and ran across the green, making for the barracks to warn his mother.

Though the night was blacker than ever, fear lit his path.

Behind him he could hear his father's pounding boots.

Passing the Methodist chapel the congregation were emerging. He whimpered past them, his thin legs moving hopelessly as in a nightmare.

Glancing over his shoulder he saw his father's flash-lamp slashing at the dark and heard his mad profanity to the Methodists.

'Outa fuck outa me way!'

His father rarely swore. This was life or his mother's death.

When he burst into the kitchen she was sitting by the range knitting.

'He's coming ... the money ... he's coming ... Tully ... Daddy's coming to kill you.'

She stood, worry in her eyes, her hand across her mouth in surprise, a weak smile of shame on her face.

The secret was out.

His father's salary arrived each month and on the kitchen table was divided into ivy-green pounds and ten-shilling notes the colour of a robin's breast. He was mean with money, never giving her enough, the best part of it being locked away in the black box under his bed, where it stayed until he took it with him, every six months, to the bank in Cavan.

His mother was always afraid to ask for more. Only she and Tully knew how much her debts had mounted. £200. Men robbed post offices for less.

Exhausted by fear, the boy flung himself into the armchair, burying his face in the hole left by his father's fist.

His mother lifted him and held him.

'Run, Mammy, run.'

Outside, his father fumbled in mad anger at the doorknob.

When he charged into the kitchen his face was sweaty with murderous rage.

'You hung me high, you hopeless bitch, and yes you know it!'

Notebook in hand he swiped at her but the boy jumped in his way, receiving the slap of the book on the side of his head.

'And you, you little maggot. Like a nail in a shoe. In me way every step I take.'

He started bawling, looking into his father's face, hoping to distract him. But instead of running out, his mother stood by the dresser, almost inviting doom.

'You never give me enough money. Every item in that book is food or what we badly needed.'

'Shut up, you never asked me, you've made me out a dolt to the world at large.'

In a swoon of rage he waved his fists, kicked the

furniture, tore off his greatcoat, spat on the range, bared his teeth, implored with rolling eyes the picture of the Sacred Heart.

'Half a year's salary. Two hundred pounds. Two hundred pounds. Two hundred fecking pounds!'

His intonation crescendoed to utter bafflement. He looked comic. Only a short while ago he was boasting he didn't owe any man one penny.

His mother's face was brave and hopeless.

There was no one to help her. Outside, the wind tore the trees and the cruel hills pressed round the barracks. They were hopelessly lost, cut off from the rest of the world.

He stood between them on the accustomed ground of love and hate. The frightened tenderness of his mother and the mad passion of his father were far beyond his power. He was about as useful as a moth.

Hands outstretched on the mantelpiece, feet straddled, rump sticking across the kitchen, his father groaned like a sick animal.

The boy looked to his mother. Bravely she winked at him and smiled to give him courage.

Then his father, as if aware of his ridiculous posture, straightened himself and turned to stare at them. He appeared calmer, but his mouth was dangerously tight, his eyes half closed.

Frightened, the boy went to his mother. She smiled her innocent smile of martyrdom and when the tears rolled down her cheeks, his father seemed to soften but then plunged himself to wild blindness. Going to the table he flung it away from the wall. Hanging above the tilley lamp was the rifle. He shot rabbits with it on summer evenings on the hills along the border.

His mother screamed.

'Daddy, Daddy.'

The boy tried to shout but the words died in his throat. He didn't know whether he was fainting or the world had stopped. His father's hand reaching up to get the gun seemed in slow motion.

Resting on the rifle butt was the moth. To the boy it appeared big and horrible and its tongue was poking out at him. Like in a bad dream.

Disturbed, it zigged crazily about his father's head, then dived down into the globe of the tilley lamp.

He could see its great dark shadow beating at the coloured glass and the dust flying out the top.

His father turned with the rifle and was pulling the bolt back when the trapped moth crashed into the mantle, instantly crumbling it.

In the darkness his mother escaped out the door.

For a second the boy thought he had awoken from a nightmare, then he found himself following his father from room to room, as, torch in hand, he opened and closed wardrobes, cupboards, looked under beds, searched everywhere, even, in his madness, looking into a commode. But she was nowhere to be found.

The boy went outside and called to her.

His bleats were lost in the night. Crossing the road, he climbed up a broken part of the demesne wall and sat there, waiting, listening. He was no longer afraid of the dark. The dark was calm, furry and kept him safe.

Footsteps approached along the road. High heels.

'Mammy, Mammy, don't go in, he wants to kill you.'

Startled, a young woman answered him. 'What's that?'

Feeling foolish, he got down from his perch and crossed back over into the barracks.

Peeping in the kitchen window, he saw his father slumped in the armchair, one hand shading his eyes. An oil lamp burned on the sewing machine and the rifle was back on the wall.

He went round to the back of the barracks, to the sheds.

'Mammy, Mammy.'

'I'm here, darling.'

They sat together in the oil house, which had a bolt on the inside of the door. The oil house was bare, save for a barrel of paraffin raised on blocks and a measuring can on a bench under the tap. They sat on the bench, sharing an old greatcoat of his father's which she had managed to grab on her way out.

'What are we going to do, Mammy?'

'Nothing. He'll be sorry in the morning.'

'How do you know?'

'That's the way it is.'

Mantled in his father's greatcoat he thought of all the creatures he knew, those that scuttled, those that flew and decided that his favourite was definitely the moth. Especially a big yellow one recently dead.

'Can an insect be a ghost?'

'No. He'll go to the bank in the morning, get the

money and that'll be the end for Tully. How well he couldn't keep the secret. Men.'

'But how were you going to pay the money, Mammy?'

'I don't know. I was hoping my luck might change.'

She chuckled, then sighed.

He cuddled into her and pressed his face in past the buttons of her blouse.

'No, you mustn't. You're not a baby any more.' He persisted.

She began singing, softly. 'Oh youth of France prepare yourselves for war . . .'

Soft as a moth landing on silk, his lips found her nipple and her arms cradling him were wings flying him to the warmest spot in the world.

OUT

THE CLOCK ON THE kitchen wall was tockless. From the hallway he could hear the escaping tick, but somewhere in the metal guts the tock was strangled.

He had been sent out by his father.

'This is not for you to see. Wait out there.'

He was horrified by what was taking place and had shouted at his father. In a strange way, though, he was excited as well.

They were in Conlon's house. Nothing here worked properly. Doorknobs came away in your hand, damp plaster bulged from the walls and the sofa he now lay on sloped because the front castors were missing. And where else would hens be allowed into the front room? The furniture was ancient, dusty but the best.

'Them chairs is Chippendale,' Conlon's mother had told him, 'and you see don organ – a king would give his right hand to play it.'

The organ, big as a wardrobe, had rows of stop-knobs, some of them with the names of musical instruments, and on either side of the music-rest were brass candle-sticks, on one of which Conlon hung his hat when sitting down to play.

It was the only time he ever removed his hat and the way he bowed his head before commencing and from the look on his face, the boy guessed he was full of sad and bitter memories.

Wellington boots removed, he worked the pedals in stockinged feet, the throbbing music crashing through the house and swelling the winter gloom to bursting point.

Sometimes when he played, the bull on the hill at the back of the house ran down to the gate, dunting it and bellowing madly, so that old Mrs Conlon was terrified it was going to break out.

'Stop, George, stop – the bull, the bull!'

'Aye, Mother, bulls first, music second. We're an agri-cultural country after all.'

The gate was two iron bed-heads and a sheet of galvanise lashed to a wooden frame.

Conlon had never married. Engaged once, the boy had heard it said that his intended bride, when she saw the bull looking down on her from the hill through the kitchen window, eyes inflamed, longing to gore her, fled back to her family in the Country Cork, leaving her engagement ring in the letter-box wrapped in a farewell note and never again set foot in Butlershill.

Others put the blame on old Mrs Conlon, a stern-looking person of eighty who still rode her bicycle about the village, a gamp clutched across the handlebars. The gamp she used to wallop Agnew's cur when it came alongside trying to bite the long black cloak she wore and which flapped behind her like a torn sail.

After his father's row with Tully it was decided that the boy would in future get the milk from Conlon's. The first evening he walked up the drive to the house he felt he knew what to expect.

But as soon as he opened the high galvanised gate into the yard a sow, moving with a dull waddle, a regiment of tits swinging angrily from its belly, made straight to attack him.

A bull he was prepared for; no one however had mentioned a mad pig. His father had warned him about sows.

'In the animal kingdom, there's none would munch a youngster quicker.'

'Why, Daddy?'

'Tormented by its litter, it maybe sees a child as yet another, even bigger mouth to feed.'

The sow was getting nearer. He had time to escape. He could see the tits hanging like cups from its belly, dragging through the deep mud, slowing it down. But he couldn't move.

Standing in a shed doorway, staring at him, horrifying him to stupor, was a man with eyes clear as Christ in a hobgoblin body twisted out of shape.

The man's cropped head was locked to one shoulder, back hunched, legs knock-kneed, feet inwards and his mouth a crooked gash sloping past his chin.

Buckets hung heavily from his wrists, held in place by upturned claws of knotted fingers.

A string of spit dribbled from his mouth to the lapel of his jacket.

The approaching sow was bad enough but this creature was more frightening than a nightmare devil.

Grunting and bending he stepped from the shed doorway into the muck of the yard. Knees jerking, head juddering, arms anchored by the heavy buckets, he began moving towards the boy.

As each foot came out of the muck, it hung for a moment before squelching down again, so that between steps he seemed balanced in a dream of motion, like a statue coming to life or crumbling to pieces. The angry sow was only feet away but the boy couldn't move, couldn't cry for help.

The twisted man grunted fiercely. The sow stopped, turned and drove at him, almost knocking him over to get at the food in the buckets. The man looked over at him. His face was stubbled but his eyes were clear and blue like the willow pattern on a plate.

'Ughod oy. Ughod oy . . .'

The boy knew he was trying to speak to him but the words came out strangled into breathy, senseless groans, sounding as horrible as he looked.

The man had saved him from the angry sow but he couldn't thank him. He just wanted to be out of his sight. But there was no going back without the milk. Liquid manure swilling over his shoes and socks, he cut round to the back of the house and in the open door of

Conlon's kitchen. Conlon's mother was in an armchair, her leg resting on a dog stretched out in front of the fire.

Her leg was bare, long and thin and the boy could see running sores along the shin-bone. Weeping green and red with pus and blood. She sat staring into the flames and like the dog unaware of his presence.

Her hair was grey and scragged up in a bun.

The dog lay flat along the cement floor, its tattered ears spread on either side of its head like empty gloves.

Dog and woman were very old.

When he cleared his throat they shifted their heads in unison and looked at him. In the silence the clock ticked, somewhere in its guts the tock strangled.

The dog, head down, limped over to him and with effort jumped to lick his face.

'Down, Teddy. You must be the Sergeant's son. Come here 'til I see you.'

Her long bony fingers felt his face and under his chin.

In the corner a clocken hen stood up, stretched her wings and fluffing her feathers settled back down on her eggs.

The dog lay by the fire and sighed when the old woman rested her leg on its back.

'What are you frikened of?'

'Nothing. Where's the tock?'

'It's bunged this years. It needs cleanin' out. Wee face on you like a scaldie. How is Mammy? She's one lady. And a great waltzer.'

The boy knew his mother was a good dancer, despite her varicosed legs. Sometimes his father grabbed her and swung her round the kitchen to a wireless tune. She was light on her feet, her black high heels slipping in and out between his father's boots, her face annoyed when his knees hit her thighs.

'Don't bend your knees like that for heaven's sake.'

'What? We need space.'

'Keep time. One-two-three. One-two-three . . .'

The boy dragged the armchair to the side and watched them struggle for rhythm round the kitchen, his father's big hand on her back, the thumb hooked in the buttoned gap of her frock.

The lino ticked and crinkled under them and every time they hit the corner of the dresser, crockery clacked like false teeth.

The silver buckle of his father's belt swung out from his uniform jacket when they executed sudden turns and his mother let her head back in laughter, her creamy neck curving in the golden light.

'That's it, that's enough. Stop.'

'No, come on, carry on, you're moving lovely.'

When his father was happy, his mother felt safe enough to sting him.

'Sit down, sit down. You've walked all over me. You're like a bull at a gate. Dear oh dear oh dear. There was a time I could dance.'

'There was a time we never stopped.'

They sat drinking from a mug of water and the boy looked at the flesh of his mother's insteps bulging above the rims of her shoes. Sometimes she cried for her legs.

'Look at them. Plain as pounders. They're not the legs

I grew up with at all. Sometimes I feel they're going to burst like balloons. God help me what did I do to deserve this?'

'Now, now, that's enough. They're all right. Rest them, amn't I always telling you?'

'You can't rest and waltz at the same time.'

She always resolved never to dance again but when she heard music her feet itched and every year when the carnival came to the village green they went to the Ceilidhe and Old Time held on Sunday afternoons for parents and their children.

It was at the carnival they met George Conlon.

Because of Conlon's age and circumstance none of the girls would dance with him and married women hid behind their husbands if they saw him approach.

At a 'Ladies' Choice' his mother had taken pity on him and asked him to dance.

The boy stood on a chair and watched them move into the centre of the packed marquee.

Trapped in the press of bodies they twirled round and round and round, caught like leaves in the whirlpool of an old-time waltz.

His father laughed.

'The cut of him – dancing with his hat on.'

The boy sensed danger. Such was the crush on the dance floor, Conlon was tight to his mother and his face touched her face and they were the same height and, despite his hat and shabby suit, his weather-beaten face and eyes were sad and his mother smiled gently all the time the music played.

'Get down off that chair, you!'

He sat. His father stood beside him, his foot tapping a methodical rhythm of its own.

The dance ended and his mother came back to them alone.

'You're not jealous are you, surely to God?'

'Who said I was?'

'Poor Conlon. Smelt of hay and cigarette smoke.'

'You were close enough to sniff.'

His mother's happy mood crumbled and she sat with a despairing bump on one of the forms running round the canvas walls of the marquee. Her insteps pouted from her shoes like swollen lips.

A bead of perspiration truckled her powdered cheek.

Her blue frock was sleeveless and when his father dragged her by the upper arm to her feet, the boy glimpsed the damp pit of hair, blackish brown and glistening like wet turf.

'You're dancing with me now!'

When his father was angry, the skin tightened on his face, his eyes and cheekbones glinting like flint.

Leading her to the dance floor as if she were under arrest, he knocked people out of the way with his rump and shoulders.

Clutching the back of his mother's frock, the boy followed in their wake.

Reaching the centre of the floor, they came face to face with Conlon. He was leaning against a marquee pole, his hat slicing a shadow across his eyes, a cigarette dangling in the corner of his lips.

'I know little about you, Sergeant, but I'll say one thing – your wife is the first lady come in the village since the day my fiancée went out of it. I hear you've taken the field next to the barracks. You'll be wantin' to plough. You can have a loan of our mare any day you want.'

A smile ripped slowly across his father's face. When he released his grip the boy saw the blood blush the finger tracks on his mother's arm.

His father's mood was changing. He was getting something for nothing.

'Well now, that's very kind of you indeed, George, a very generous offer. Isn't it?'

The boy could see his mother's anger. She didn't reply but swayed forward slightly to shake off the arm encircling her waist.

'Dance if we're dancing.'

'Hold your horses. These young fillies, you have to keep a tight rein on them, George.'

He laughed in high good humour, charm oozing from him. When he was happy he seemed to swell and get more handsome. He was in his civvies – blue open-necked shirt, dark tweed jacket, light flannel trousers and on his feet second-hand dress shoes which he found in a wardrobe he bought at an auction. They were still stylish despite the wrinkled toecaps and the soles thick with repairs, like his police boots.

When they began waltzing, his mother hung in his arms, lifeless as a stook of corn. She was punishing him and held her head back so their cheeks wouldn't touch. His father was lifting her around the floor, shoving her backwards, twisting her to the sides, clutching her close to him, holding her at arms' length, all the time smiling, pretending they were at one with each other and the music.

The boy followed in their wake, lost in a meadow of flapping trousers, swishing frocks, clacking shoes and nylons held up with garters and suspenders which he saw when the girls spun to show their legs. They spun freely at first, showing hunks of pale flesh, then stopped abruptly, snapping their dresses about them, hiding everything.

Above the knees his mother's legs were white and smooth. The thighs didn't have knotted veins. They were clear as butter.

Supposed to be asleep, he sometimes watched her standing for ages in the half-light by the wardrobe mirror, pinching and palping her flesh, cupping her bosom with her hands, sighing.

His father had the mystery of stone, his mother clay.

Together, struggling on the clogged dance floor, they worried him. His father sweating with her unhappiness, her bitter look draining his false smile.

When they saw him following them, they stopped in amazement.

'What's the matter, darling? Come here.'

'Always where he isn't wanted. Off home with you now. Before you're trampled on by these clodhoppers.'

The marquee heaved like a stomach and the dancers were coils of gut and he had to fight his way down through them to the exit, where Conlon stood, smiling at him, raising the flap to let him pass.

All that day and night and days after, his mother and

father were in silence and he went between them with curt requests, refusals, commands.

'Tell him his tea is ready.'

'Tell her I don't want any.'

'Tell him his egg will be hard.'

'Tell her the egg isn't the only thing round here hard boiled.'

'Tell him it takes two to fight.'

'Tell her she should know. And here, me buck, what's a ruminating animal?'

'A cud chewer.'

'How many stomachs has a cow?'

'Four?'

'Yes, yes. What's your intestine?'

'Belly gut.'

'Goodnight. Good boy.'

'Goodnight, Daddy. Goodnight, Mammy.'

'Goodnight, darling. I'll be with you soon.'

'Yes. And when will you be with me?'

The days and nights died in silence.

Conlon sent the mare, they ploughed the field and that evening as he lay in bed he heard them talking and then coming down the hallway and going into his father's room.

The door, swollen with damp, closed with its familiar scrape and final thump.

A month later Conlon called to the barracks with a bag of cabbage. The boy lugged it round to the married quarters and emptied it on to the kitchen floor.

'The best, the best,' said his father, 'look at the tight hearts in them.'

On every leaf wet diamonds sparkled.

'Fresh as morning. That Ladies' Choice was the best move you ever made.'

'Pity you didn't think so at the time.'

'Yes and if we could see round corners cars wouldn't need horns.'

The last word was gold to his father. As good as blood.

Conlon, at first a joke, was now a family friend.

The boy knew he was a lonely man. He saw him sometimes standing at the corner of Tully's shop, always on his own, always smoking. Under the brim of his hat his eyes were watery, his sharp face pinched by the weather, the night closing around him, the cigarette glowing occasionally like a lamp lost in wilderness.

The boy knew he lived with his mother but until that first evening he went for the milk, no one had ever told him about the twisted man.

The ulcers on Conlon's mother's leg were disgusting but the boy moved to her to escape the grunting and the crooked shadow struggling across the muck outside the back door.

'Don't be frikened. It's only Harry.'

She turned her head to the door, so did the dog and in silence they waited, the boy shivering with fright.

A splash of mud, a twisted leg, a knot of fingers hooked on the jamb of the door, a grunt and the man stood before them.

'Uh heh eee.'

'The Sergeant's lad come for the milk.'

'Ughod oy. Ughod oy.'

Twisting his head to his shoulder he wiped the string of dribble hanging from his mouth on to his jacket.

'Say hello to Harry. Go on. Say hello.'

'Heh . . . hello.'

The man held his hand out and the boy went cold at the thought of having to shake it.

'He wants the can.'

He went to him and hung the handle across his wrist.

In an agony of crazy motion, a mad slow dance, he moved to the corner of the kitchen where a white enamelled pail stood, full to the brim with milk.

'Infantight paralysis. From the day he was born. Scoured the country for cures. To no avail. A tinker woman told me the day he went into hospital would be his last day. Thank God he's never had to, in forty years. You're a lucky wee lad, aren't you? The thin shanks of you. I bet you can skip like a butterfly.'

The man shook the boy's can from his wrist, clattering it on to the floor the right way up and with a strangled moan lifted the milk pail. Spell-bound, the boy watched the milk trembling but somehow not spilling, until it poured down in a twisted gush into the can on the floor.

Only a single drop of milk spilt, landing on the man's instep.

A kitten shot out from under the dresser to lick it but put off by the muck on the man's wellington went back in under the dresser again.

'Harry can remember anything. Acks him a date.

125

Acks him does he mind the time the bull broke out? Or the date the Queen got married? Go on, acks him!'

'Which Queen?'

'There's only one – the Queen of England!'

'This is Ireland.'

'The Free State – Ireland? Worse move we ever made, coming down here.'

'Why did you?'

'George had notions of grandeur. He thought it might get him a wife. We sold our sixty acres of flat Fermanagh land for eighty acres of Cavan hills. And still none of the bitches would come near him. God help him.'

Her lips were thin, tight, sour. The boy was sorry for her. She was old and her leg shone with pain. He decided to ask the man a question.

'What year was the All-Ireland final played in New York?'

'He's not interested in football. Acks him a history question. Go on.'

The man stood looking at him, his mouth slobbering again, his eyes wide and waiting.

'When did the Queen get married?'

He began to wheeze and wind himself up to answer but before he could do so Conlon came in the glass-panelled door from the hallway to the kitchen.

Going to the mantelpiece he took from a vase a half-smoked cigarette and from his hatband a match, which he struck along the hardened surface of his trousers. Sucking the smoke deep, he stared at his mother's leg, then went out the back door.

His movements were quick, sharp and so were his words to the twisted man.

'Out, you, and throw some food at the hens.'

The local accent was flat, dry, gnarled but people like the Conlons from across the Border, only a mile away, were thorny-tongued, curt, cutting. His mother and father were from the West, their accents soft, lilting, their misty mouths dripping with double meanings.

Words were garters. They held truth up but could also be twisted, played on, whanged home to hurt.

The boy watched the twisted man trying to hasten out the door to do as was bid. His arms and legs flailing in panic, he reminded him of a bird trapped in oil.

Not only did the twisted man work – he was expected to!

'It's not fair.'

Conlon's mother rolled her bony index finger along her festering leg.

'If life was fair, nettles wouldn't sting.'

The man reaching the door hooked himself to the jamb and twisted out into the mucky yard.

'How does he shave and wash?'

Conlon's mother laughed.

'George has to do it every Saturday night. Away off home now. You've dandered long enough. These ulsters are killing me poor leg. And the one in me stomich is no better.'

Ulsters. Stomich. Dandered. He knew what she meant but he didn't know the meaning of infantight paralysis. He'd ask his father. His father knew words and how to use them like a truncheon. Before going to sleep most nights, he read *The Sacred Heart Messenger*, animal adventure stories in *The Wide World* or definitions in his *'Police-Duty' Catechism and Reports*. Strange words he underlined with a puce pencil and next day looked up their meanings in the dictionary.

'Words are like money – the more you have, the richer you are. Though how so many thundering fools end up with piles in the bank beats me.'

He said goodby to Mrs Conlon, the dog, the clocken hen, the kitten peeping at him from under the dresser and went into the yard and round the gable end of the house to the galvanised gate.

The twisted man was in the empty bay of a tumble-down hayshed, feeding hens from a huge iron pot hanging from his wrist. The hens flocking his feet, when he scattered the mash of corn and potatoes, a good deal of it landed on top of their backs where it stuck to the feathers like lumps of glue.

As he closed the galvanised gate behind him, the man groaned and grunted loudly after him.

'Een edded entee uhimber ointee uhnid en ortee evenn. Ughod oy.'

His parents weren't in when he got home. On the table was a scrawled note from his mother saying they had gone out for a walk. He put the can of milk in the meat-safe and went to bed.

But he was no sooner under the covers when the twisted man appeared before him. When he shut his eyes he could still see him. The horrible twisted body shocking him, the eyes calming him, like the eyes of Christ in the thorny picture hanging above the bed. He got right down under the blankets, counted to fifty, pretended he was sucking a lollipop, hummed the 'Marseillaise', thought of Santa Claus . . . but it was no use. When he came up for air the man was still there – a twisted, crouching scarecrow of shadow, wardrobe and flickering light.

If you didn't understand something, it kept appearing to you.

Jumping out of bed he ran up to the kitchen. For a second he thought he was dreaming. The table was out in the middle of the floor and his father was chasing his mother around it. Her face was flushed and he didn't know whether she was giggling or crying. His father's braces were hanging round his rump and his shirt was out over the front of his trousers.

'What the hell are you doing here?'

His father dived at him but he skipped round the table to his mother.

'What's infantight paralysis?'

'Did you have a nightmare, darling?'

'Harry Conlon. He's down in the room trying to get into the wardrobe.'

'Don't be bleddy thick. Go back to bed at once.'

'But what's infantight?'

'Infantile! Infantile paralysis! What about it?'

'It's something happens when you're born. You grow up deformed. Like poor Harry. Now back to bed quick, darling, and you with nothing on your feet.'

'But why does it happen?'

His father wedging his shirt back into his trousers angrily rapped the leg of the table with his boot.

'The stork bleddywell drops you on your head when he's delivering you. That's infantile paralysis! You're banjaxed from that day on. Now get back to bed and quit dogging our footsteps from sun up to sun down or you'll feel the heel of my hand on your lilywhite arse and I'm not joking. Now hop it!'

'For goodness sake he's old enough to know there's no such thing as the stork. The baby coming out of the womb gets clogged up and can't get free. The spine is injured and you grow up a cripple.'

'Could I get it? Could it happen to me?'

His father, grinding his teeth, turned to the picture of the Sacred Heart above the mantelpiece, his eyes screwed up in rage and reverence.

'How in the name of weeping Jesus could it happen to you? You're a good few years out of the womb, aren't you? You hopeless gaum! Though I'm beginning to have my serious doubts.'

'Leave the child alone. Come on, darling, I'm going to bed now too.'

His father blocked her way to the door but grabbing the boy by the shoulder flung him out into the hallway.

He went down to the bedroom but shut his eyes as soon as he went in the door. He didn't want to see the twisted man, whom he felt sure was sitting on the end of the bed, waiting for him.

Arms outstretched, his bare feet feeling the worn patches in the lino, he made his blind way across the room. When his fingers touched the dressing table mirror the glass felt as cold as the lino.

Only when he plucked at the silver buttons on one of his father's greatcoats, thrown across the bed as an extra blanket, did he feel safe enough to open his eyes.

In the deeper dark beneath the covers he lay still, hardly daring to breathe.

The silence hummed in his ears, then shattered. In the kitchen his father was shouting.

'Yes, yes, yes. Or do you want to drive me mad entirely?'

Each word had his father in it. The grinding teeth, the snarl of rage, the curdling lilt.

He lay listening. Then he felt a weight pressing the bed, sitting on his feet.

'Ughod oy. Ughod oy.'

'Go away, Harry. I want to sleep. Go away.'

When he awoke it was morning and he was in his mother's arms. Looking at her sleeping face he prayed she would live for ever. She was hope, safety, warmth, love, breakfast, dinner and tea.

But he knew come evening he would have to fetch the milk and face the twisted man again. He would have to face him every single evening from now on.

As he approached Conlon's for the second time, the man had grown so monstrously in his imagination he dreaded opening the gate into the yard. He stood outside for a few minutes, listening, but when he couldn't hear his grunts and shufflings decided it was safe enough to stand on his tiptoes and peep through that part of the galvanised gate cut out round the iron latch. The yard was empty. Relieved, he opened the gate and went in.

As if pushed, he clanged back in shock against the galvanise.

The twisted man was there, at the other end of the yard, on his hands and knees at the entrance to a byre. It looked as if he had fallen over and was trapped in the mud. In the distance he was like an animal with clothes on.

The boy, waiting for the man to make even a slight move, overcame his fear and moved slowly across the yard to get a closer look.

Drawing nearer he could see that the man was twisted over something. Whatever it was, the man was lying on top of it. It was something bulky and pinkish and to the boy's horror seemed to be alive and the man's knotted hand was stroking it.

Now it didn't seem as if the man had fallen at all. Something else was happening. Fear seeping all over him, he inched closer.

Having rained for days the cow dung in the yard was deep and liquid green. And the man was kneeling in it. Doing something.

Opposite the byre was a concrete water-tank, an abandoned plough alongside, the rusty handles curving up from the muck in which the mould-boards lay buried. Not wanting the dung to spill in over the tops of his wellingtons, he made for the plough and stood on it, his feet on the frame, his back against the water-tank. From there he could see clearly what was going on.

It was the angry sow. Lying at the entrance to the byre, the twisted man was on his hands and knees beside it. The boy couldn't understand why he was like that and why the sow was breathing heavily as if dying.

Then to his amazement the sow's rear gaped open, as if ripping, and something white squelched out of it on to the ground. Whatever it was it looked disgusting and then the twisted man knuckled it round to the sow's tits, when it seemed to come alive and stood on legs and had a snout which latched on to a nipple with such ferocity, the sow grunted and tried to turn its head to look.

Then the rear opened again and out popped another piglet, this one coming immediately to its feet and receiving a nudge from the twisted man went tottering to its mother's belly.

The twisted man stroked the sow, his knotted fingers trembling and scratching along its fat back and every time the sow grunted the twisted man grunted, so it appeared to the boy that man and animal were having a conversation.

The sow's rear pulsing open and shut was hypnotic and he got down from the plough and went right over to have a closer look.

'Ughod oy.'

It was a blind, weeping eye, widening to bloody life. A lippy slit, blinking out slimy sausages, each with a snout and legs.

Soon there were ten of them, all blindly sucking the sow.

When next the slit opened the sow began to grunt and whack its head on the ground and instead of a snout appearing first, the boy could see a tiny tail, back legs, then the body and lastly the head. It seemed bigger than the others but somehow couldn't get properly to its feet. Quivering with effort it tried to drag itself forward but the boy could see it was deformed. He wanted to help it but the twisted man hit it with the back of his crooked hand, knocking it from the dry ground of the byre entrance into the liquid manure of the yard. It drowned, shivering, in the dung.

The man looked at the boy and tried to calm him with his eyes but the boy turned and fled to Conlon's kitchen for help.

'Come quick, come quick. Something's happening. One is dead. The twisted man drowned it!'

Mrs Conlon was limping round the kitchen with a sweeping brush. Her height startled him, her black dress, buttoned all the way down the front, hanging on her like a scarecrow's overcoat. Her ulcerated leg was bare, the stocking on the other one loose about her skinny ankle. She was as tall as his father.

'Move yer bones!'

The dog shifting from the fire, she swept a drift of dirt and dust into the ashes.

'You mind your tongue, wee lad. Harry's his name. I told ye before!'

'It couldn't walk when it came out. Was it infantile paralysis? He killed it in the mud. Harry!'

'The sow's piggin', that's all. Harry knows what to do. How many is there so far?'

'Ten.'

'Run out and see how many now.'

He raced across the yard and began counting the nuzzling bodies. They were as alike as thumbs of pastry and he had difficulty working out how many there were.

'Efeen. Efeen.'

For the first time he understood the twisted man. Fifteen. And the slit was opening again and out came the sixteenth as easy as toothpaste from a tube. Slithering to its feet it slipped and slid to the others and blindly clambered over them until it latched on to a nipple halfway along the uppermost row of tits.

As each one arrived he ran in to Mrs Conlon with the news. Sixteen. Seventeen. Eighteen. He was amazed the sow's belly could hold so many. Nineteen. Twenty. His excitement grew to a pitch, matched by the old woman's delighted laughter.

'The wee runty face of you. It's the best sport I've had for years. Go back and see if there's another.'

When he announced the twenty-first she rocked with laughter in her chair.

' "There's *another* one," ' she mimicked him, 'if only George was here. "There's *another* one." You're as good as a concert. Away home now or Mammy won't know what's happened ye.'

It was raining as he went out through the yard and the twisted man was crouched over the sow and her litter, a hessian sack stretched across his arms, giving them shelter. Behind Conlon's the hill sheered higher than the house and hayshed and over the top of it the rain came pelting down into the yard, churning the green muck, cutting into the twisted man's face, soaking his humped back.

When he closed the gate behind him, he peeped through the gap round the latch. The twisted man never flinched in the downpour. He was hunched rigid in his task of sheltering the pigs. In the fading light he looked like a slab of stone roughly chipped in the resemblance of a man.

'Ughod oy.'

He went home wondering what those noises meant but he believed he now knew the meaning of infantile paralysis and he also knew storks definitely had nothing to do with birth. Life came out a slit but how it got in there he wasn't quite sure.

His wellington boots were filled with squelching dung which had spilled in unnoticed as he ran to and from the kitchen.

Stopping to empty them he looked across the village green and saw the glow of a cigarette. Night was down but he knew it was George Conlon, rooted to his customary spot by the gable end of Tully's. He stood there escaping his mother, his twisted brother, the bull, the sow, the tumbledown sheds, the mucky yard, the chickens perched on the Chippendale chairs down in the cool front room and the crocked tractor, headlights smashed, standing in the haggard like a great blind frog.

The boy knew that's what happened if you failed to

get a wife. The world half stopped or the tock went missing like the clock in Conlon's kitchen. The same thing would happen if your mother left you. To drown the fear he prayed frantically, rattling off a string of Hail Marys and Our Fathers, but as he went in the barracks' gate he noticed his fingers and thumbs were cocked like pistols and he was in the middle of rounding up a party of bandits along the Mexican border. It was always the same when he prayed. He started out holy but without fail ended up in a gun battle or sometimes in a saloon bar with Wild West honky-tonk music playing in his head. On the whole, praying was fun.

Every Friday when he went to Conlon's he took money with him to pay for the week's supply of milk. On two successive Fridays Conlon wouldn't take the money so the boy's mother to repay his generosity invited him to Sunday tea.

Almost as soon as he came into the kitchen Conlon began talking about marriage and the boy noticed his father's secret smile when he sat down to table without removing his hat.

'I've had women interested all right. But as soon as they came to the house and met me mother and Harry . . . they never came back.'

'I doubt you'll get a wife now, George. At this late stage,' said his father bluntly.

Conlon bit the end of a scallion and glanced at the boy.

'To have a farm and no one to pass it on to! A house and no cry in it but chickens, kittens, dogs and pigs! A grand spread this, missus. Best homemade bread I tasted since . . . since a certain girl came to the house, years ago, and baked a batch of loaves for us.'

At the end of the meal the boy knew he was going to be sent out and told to play but he sneaked back in and listened at the keyhole.

'Up until the day she came to the house she never said one cross word. We went to dances. Everything. She and Mother right enough didn't hit it off . . . But what was I to do – walk out on me mother? I went down to Cork after her but she wouldn't come back.'

'Might be all for the best. It's no good forcing them. Marriage is a knot you tie with your hands you can't undo with your teeth,' said his father.

'It's not fair,' said his mother. 'It's not fair.'

'I'll be honest with you, Sergeant, I've often thought of biting the end of me shotgun.'

The boy heard his father's knife clatter to his plate and a deadly silence fell over the whole house.

He imagined their anguished faces and he longed to be in with them but he stayed at the keyhole, breathing quietly and waiting for words to come.

Bottles clunked, a cork popped and at last his father spoke.

'Good God, man, don't dare even think about it!'

'It's not fair,' said his mother. 'It's not fair.'

'The only thing stops me is Harry. What would happen to him?'

'Indeed, indeed. God bless us this night.'

'One cartridge, that's all it would take.'

'That's enough now, George. Suicide is out of the question. Not in my sub-district!'

His mother was the first to laugh, then Conlon and the boy unable to restrain himself opened the door and joined them. His father, angry with them at first, slowly realised how ludicrous and selfish his words were and he too started laughing. Soon his mother was on her knees weeping hysterically and as his father was lifting her Conlon said – 'Leave her, Sergeant. While she's down there she may as well say a decade of the Rosary.'

This started them off again and they didn't stop until Agnew's cur came barking to the door.

Conlon was odd. He was honest about his feelings, smiled though in despair and took his hat off only when he played the organ down in the cool front room of his house, where eggs were incubated on the oak table and hens perched on the backs of the Chippendale chairs.

In summer he hired labourers to save the hay and the boy ran errands for them. He fetched cuds of tobacco for The Boxer Duffy, cigarettes and chocolate for Joe 'The Nut' Fay and at lunchtime cans of sweet tea and hunks of bread and cheese for them all.

In between times his main job was helping the twisted man carry cans of cold drink to the men, up the steep hill at the back of the house. It was bad enough walking beside him in the yard with the muck baked into uneven lumps by the sun but climbing the hill was a nightmare in daytime.

The twisted man's legs jerked up, down and sideways, his arms flailed for balance and though the rise of the hill stopped him tottering forwards, sometimes when they paused for breath the force of the hill seemed to grab him by his hump and topple him cruelly backwards.

'Oree. Oree.'

He hated trying to get him upright. He had to touch him and take his clawed hands and drag him trembling to his feet and stand there while he leaned on him until he steadied himself and was able to turn and face the slope again. When he was being leant on he was always terrified the spittle stringing from his mouth was going to fall on his head.

'Ughod oy. Ughod oy.'

Then he had to run back down to the kitchen, re-fill the twisted man's bucket, go back up the hill and face his blue eyes sad and smiling.

'Oree. Ughod oy.'

And when eventually they came into the hayfield the men always cheered.

'At last. The fastest pair on earth. Master McGrath couldn't keep up with them.'

'A fellah could a died of the drought waitin'. What kept you, gauson – did you take a short cut through Belturbet?'

Though he didn't like being linked with the twisted man he was angry on his behalf.

'Why does Harry have to do anything? It's not fair.'

'On a farm all animals work.'

The reply was bitter but the boy could see from Conlon's face it was as much against himself as against his brother.

Conlon's farm was eighty acres of hill, bog and rock. And the one flat meadow was for most of the year a swamp.

The men lay drinking the water mixed with meal, their hayforks pronged into the ground beside them.

The handles of the forks, smooth from use, gleamed like police batons. Way below them the village green and the white houses of Butlershill lay in the heat dead as spilt paint.

'Ay,' said The Boxer Duffy, flapping with his cap at a red spider running up his arm, 'if you haven't the money to drink yourself to death you're as well off working. It's either that or die bored. Doesn't matter who you are – cripple or cured.'

Joe The Nut Fay broke squares of chocolate and gave them all one each and the boy watched the twisted man munch it and the slobber from his mouth turn slowly brown.

'Do you follow football?' Conlon asked.

'I do,' answered the boy.

'Do you follow God?'

'I do.'

Conlon's eyes cut into him from under the brim of his hat.

'You might change your tune when you start to follow the girls.'

'Do you believe in a United Ireland, seeing as you're the Sergeant's son, I'd like to know, you know?' The Boxer Duffy spoke to him without looking at him.

'Quit teasing him,' said Joe The Nut Fay, 'he's only a gauson.'

'Fuck you,' said The Boxer dangerously, 'I'd like to know what you believe in, Fay, come on, tell us!'

In the hot silence they waited for Fay's reply.

Joe The Nut was afraid of The Boxer Duffy. They were all afraid of him. The boy knew the only man not afraid of him was his father.

Conlon pulled his hat even lower on his eyes but the boy could see him smiling, enjoying the tension.

'Right, I'll tell you if you want to know,' Fay said at last. 'Hairy bacon and apple pie, I'll believe in both 'til I die.'

Standing up, he pulled his fork out of the earth and flicking over swathes of hay went down the field.

Conlon chuckled. The Boxer Duffy spat in anger, the cud of spit and tobacco landing in a big juicy blob near the boy's foot.

'Fuck you. Like all Monaghan men, you believe in anythin' you get for nothin'!' His angry shout seemed to roll down the hill and land on the distant houses of the village.

'Leave him alone,' said Conlon, 'don't get your dander up so easy.'

Not until he was safely down the field did Fay speak and when he did his voice rasped abuse.

From Wattlebridge to Lisnaskea
No meaner men you'll ever see.

'Aye,' shouted The Boxer Duffy, his big face tight with rage, 'but only if some of youse are walkin' the road.'

'Come on,' said Conlon, 'work will cool your passion.'

The boy was left with the twisted man, who was struggling to get something out of his pocket. When he grunted, the boy went to him and saw between his knuckles a medal of the Blessed Virgin. His hand trembling he rubbed the sign of the cross on his forehead and then did the same to the boy.

'Odts uthur. Odts uthur.'

They went down the hill together and the boy was no longer afraid of him.

By the end of the summer he even held his wrist and every Friday he sat at the table in the kitchen and read the *Anglo-Celt* to him and Mrs Conlon.

The first time he read to them, when he finished and got up to go home the twisted man banged the table several times with his crooked hand.

'Ughod oy. Uhest oy an Uirlan.'

'He says you're a good boy. The best boy in Ireland. And so you are, you wee runt ye!'

When he was going down the drive he could hear Conlon playing the organ and soon the bull on the hill behind the house was bellowing. He said a short prayer and meant every word of it. God would have to send Conlon's fiancée back to him. As quickly as possible. Before the sheds tumbled completely, the house rotted and the Chippendale chairs fell to pieces.

That night as he lay in his mother's arms, his father came into the room and looked down on both of them. He stood jingling coins in his pocket and then without saying a word abruptly left.

The boy sensed he wanted him out of his mother's bed and on his own in the spare room.

He clung so tight to her neck she had to prise his arms away so she could get to sleep.

He dreamt of the sow and her litter and he was sitting at table with them and they were dressed like brothers and sisters and they were snapping the food from his mouth and worse they were smothering his mother in kisses so he couldn't get anywhere near her.

In a cold sweat he woke up and in the dawn light saw his mother's bare breast and nipple and though he desperately wanted to suckle her he couldn't.

He was frightened. He lay wondering why. When he turned towards her again she was looking at him, her eyes wide open.

Winter came, the baked dung in Conlon's yard softened in the rain and soon the yard was deep in slurry. The one good thing about it was the sow was unable to move quickly through it, so the boy was always able to skip round to the kitchen without it getting near him.

Winter was here but he was still in his mother's bed.

The only thing changed was the twisted man. He was ill. Each evening when he went for the milk he saw him sitting in a dark corner away from the fire. He looked lifeless and didn't grunt, twist or tremble. The boy's mother was sent for and she looked at the twisted man's face and felt his forehead.

'Have his bowels been regular, Mrs Conlon?'

'Now you're talkin'. He hasn't passed a happorth for two weeks, maybe three. Even four.'

'What? Has the doctor been?'

'Aye. He gave him a dose of medicine, said it would shift a horse. But it hasn't budged Harry. He's fillin' up with poison and I'm desperate afeered he's going to die.'

The boy could see that the twisted man's eyes no longer shone and though his skin looked sweaty the slobber from his mouth had dried up. Conlon came in from the byre carrying two pails of milk. When he placed them on the floor they lit up the dark kitchen.

'I'm going to have to do it meself,' he said to the boy's mother. 'I'm going to have to operate on him the way you'd do a sick cow. I wonder could you help me. The Sergeant maybe as well, for he'll have to be held down.'

The boy's mother looked shocked.

'Shouldn't he be taken to hospital? Doing it yourself is, it seems to me, George, a bit drastic altogether.'

'If he goes into hospital, he'll never come out,' Conlon replied with utter conviction.

'Aye,' said Mrs Conlon, 'it was prophesied that by a tinker woman came to the door when he was only a year old. He's not going to hospital and the doctor's medicine is usless. George is right.'

When next evening the boy went for the milk his mother and father were with him.

Conlon, the milking done, was waiting for them.

The boy was terrified at what they were going to do and he could see that the twisted man was terrified too.

His father taking off his greatcoat and hanging it on a nail in the door was eager to get it over and done with.

'It'll only take us a couple of minutes. I've seen it done in the old days in the West of Ireland. And no one passed any remarks about it good, bad or indifferent. You have to be cruel to be kind.'

Conlon pulled the table into the middle of the floor and lifted the twisted man on to it.

The light from the tilley directly above his head turned him yellow.

'He looks sick as a dog all right,' said his father, 'no shadow of a doubt about it.'

The boy was angry with his father. He could see that already he was relishing the unpleasant task, as if all he was doing was mending a bicycle puncture or heeling a shoe.

'We'll have to strip him,' said Conlon.

His mother turned to the fire, heaping turf on it, making sure she wasn't involved.

'I'll wet some tay,' said Conlon's mother, rising from her seat and limping to the dresser.

The twisted man moaned and flailed with his arms when Conlon tried to remove his jacket.

'Aydel. Aydel.'

His father gripped the twisted man so he couldn't move. His big hands were like eagle claws.

'Work away, George.'

'Aydel. Aydel. Ughod oy.'

The boy stood in front of his father and shouted fiercely.

'Leave him alone. Leave him alone. Leave him alone.'

'Get him out of here, the nigget. Always where he isn't wanted. Out, you whelp.'

The twisted man groaned and beat his pocket with his crooked fist.

'He wants his medal.'

Dodging a swipe from his father the boy delved his hand into the man's pocket. He found a chestnut, a chocolate wrapper, a blue plastic spiralled ring for a hen's leg and at last the medal of the Blessed Virgin.

When he slid the medal between his knuckles the twisted man went limp in his father's grip and allowed them to remove his jacket.

'I'm afeered there's going to be more rain,' said Mrs Conlon.

Horrified, the boy watched them remove the man's shirt, his father roughly pulling it up over the hump. Then they laid him down on the table, his bare chest a mangle of twisted snow-white skin and bone, the hump, big as a cow's udder, tipping his shoulders one way, his head the other.

Conlon and his father were now dragging at his wellingtons and socks.

'How old is the mongrel?' enquired his father, nodding at the dog stretched by the fire.

'That's no mongrel, Sergeant. He's as near purebred as dammit. He used to catch hares regular. Aye, man, surely. Didn't you, Teddy?'

The dog's tattered ears flicked but his head stayed along the cement floor.

'Catch hares? He did in me granny,' said his father.

'I'm telling you he did. He had a rare burst of speed.

He put teeth on the wind. I mind the day he chased a hare three counties. He riz her across the Border near Wattlebridge, flaked after her along the Fin and caught her just behind Brady's pub in Legykelly. Ojus. Bet all.'

Laughing, his father threw the twisted man's wellington and sock under the table.

'The hare in question must have been dying of old age, blind or lost a leg in a traffic accident, then.'

'Believe what you like, Sergeant. If the old brute could talk he'd tell you it was no word of a lie. Couldn't you, Teddy? Trousers now, Sergeant. You lift him and I'll pull.'

The tockless clock on the wall beat into the silence with nine whanging clacks, and dust and fluff spilled out past the pendulum.

The boy's father turned to him.

'This is not for you to see. Wait out there.'

Relieved, the boy went into the hallway. Closing the door behind him the knob came away in his hand. Struggling to put it back on, through the glass panels he saw the twisted man lying naked on the table. It looked like he was nailed to a cross but without the piece of cloth Christ had on in holy pictures.

His mother and father were staring down at the body. He heard his father's words and could see the twisted man's flesh – the flesh that hung down or stood up on the animals in the fields all around him.

'Well,' his father was saying, 'Nature was generous in that department at least.' Looking up, his mother caught him peeping in.

Ducking out of sight he went and sat on the stairs leading to the bedrooms.

When the twisted man howled, the night seemed strangled and the boy plugging his ears ran down the hallway and into the cool front room. A lamp burned in the window and a hen roosting on the back of a chair ran in behind the organ. On the music rest was an open sheet. Conlon had previously played the piece for the boy and his mother.

'It was my fiancée's favourite ... Way Down Upon The Swanee River ...'

'For a farmer you have such lovely hands, George. You're wasted here, wasted. It's not fair.'

When he unplugged his ears he couldn't hear any noises in the kitchen. He lay on the sofa, which sloped because the front castors were missing.

On the wall above him hung a portrait of Conlon's father. He had died when Conlon was only ten.

Out in the dung-clogged yard he heard the sow rooting and grunting. It was the twisted man's job to lock it in each night.

He was in the kitchen pinned to the table by his father while Conlon cleaned him out the way you cleaned a sick animal.

It was the twisted man showed him how life came out and now had shown him how life went in. It made sense. Of course. How else? He felt foolish for not realising it sooner.

When he awoke he was in his father's arms, being carried home.

He heard his mother say, 'No woman could stick it. She'd have to be better than a saint.'

His mother put him to bed, kissed him, then quickly left the room.

Almost immediately his father came in. Ripping back the bed clothes he lifted him straight out on to the floor.

'Out now. You're too big any more. Out.'

Screaming he dived down and clung to the leg of the bed. In doing so he knocked over the chamber pot, the urine spilling everywhere. His father caught him by the ankles and dragged him over the wet lino to the door.

'Mammy, Mammy.'

In the kitchen he heard his mother sobbing but she didn't come to his aid.

His father had him by a wrist and a leg and hauled him through the hallway and into the spare room.

He was shivering, twisting, trembling, his teeth chattering with fear, his soul freezing and screeching out for mercy and for warmth.

'Mammy, Mammy, help me.'

His father dumped him in the cold clothes of the iron bed and left him.

The room was black as Hell. He could smell the damp. His pyjamas soaked with urine clung to his skin.

Away in the fields along the Border a rattle of machine-gun fire ripped out and fell through the night like hail-stones.

His pillow filled with tears.

He would never sleep with his mother again. Never.

Drifting to sleep he thought he was on the hills looking down on Butlershill ... looking down on his mother, his father, on everyone and they were all clogged up at the bottom of an endless black ticking gut.

He was out. Out at last. And he was glad.

Next evening when he went for the milk the twisted man was waiting for him in the yard, smiling, a bucket hanging on a crook of wrist and fingers.

'Hello, Harry.'

'Ughod oy. Ughod oy. Ughod an.'

ARSON

THE DEMESNE WALL CURVING right into the village gave them a clear view of the house and the van parked outside. They had footholds in the crumbling stonework and clinging to the spread of ivy they watched and waited.

'What if they don't come?'

'They will. They've got on their preaching clothes.'

When the sun hit the ivy it slid off. It couldn't get a grip. Green was stronger than gold.

The door opened and Bobby Roberts came out carrying something.

'It's a harmonium. For the hymns.'

'What's he got under his chin?'

'It's a bow tie. He only wears it when he's making a journey.'

They watched him load the harmonium, then go back inside. The hall door slammed through the empty village. On the green the tethered goat cried and lay down, front first, then rump.

They slithered down the wall, ran to the van, opened the rear doors and got in. The floor was piled in straw and whiffed of pig. The driver's and passengers' seats were divided from the rest of the van by a rough partition of planks. They lay waiting, whispering.

'What if they find us?'

'They won't 'til we get there.'

'Did you have your dinner? I didn't.'

'Me neither. I've three ginger biscuits on me. And when we get there we'll buy slab toffee.'

He lay panting with fear. That morning when the priest came along the altar rails towards him he could hear his heart thump and judder. He had his mouth open and tongue out before it was necessary. He drew air over his tongue, drying it, so that when the Host was placed on it he could hold it in his mouth without getting it wet. The lids twitched over his shut eyes.

Before going to Mass he had lined his pocket with one of his father's white handkerchiefs.

He wondered had his mother noticed anything.

It was Gore Kemp put the idea in his head. But if it all went wrong and they were swept away on a tide of blood, it was his own fault. Your mind ordered the body to action. But a fist could force your mind. Flesh. He was confused. Why was he doing it? If his parents found out he'd be slaughtered. They heard voices, then the hall door slam. Tilly's high heels click-clocked on the pavement. He knew her arched feet, her black suede shoes. She pranced like a horse. Flesh had a sheen. From a light shining within.

The van shuddered when she and Bobby Roberts sat in it. The engine gasped a few times, roared and they were on their way out of the village, up over the railway bridge and out the road leading to Northern Ireland.

Light reached them through two small windows in the doors and threads of day sewed together the partition planking.

The van was old, shaky and so noisy their whispers couldn't be heard in the front. Travelling in it was, in dignity, barely a step above a horse and cart.

Gore was his friend. He came on holiday every summer to his sister Tilly, who was married to Bobby Roberts the insurance man who also sold eggs. Gore was plump, wide-shouldered, small-headed. He looked like a full hot-water bottle. His body was calm but his pink eyes never stopped hunting.

'Will we nibble a ginger?'

'Yes.'

'Then will we measure our mickeys?'

'No.'

They roamed the woods together, played in the village, peeped in windows, went into the Protestant graveyard.

The headstones there had Ypres written on them, the Somme and 'POW died in Germany'. They stuck up out of the mouthy ground like buck-teeth. But round the back of the church, where you couldn't be seen from the road, were flat ones, low-lying tombs, perfect for mickey measuring. You knelt and put your mickey on the stone and you could easily see which was the longest.

'Mine is, mine is. Look.'

'You're cheating. You're off your knees.'

'Pull the skin back and we'll rub them together.'

It was the only time Gore's eyes stopped hunting.

'Quick – the vicar!'

The Reverend Dr Maddock, in gaiters and top hat, stepped from the bushes, angrily waving his umbrella.

Gore wanted to throw stones at him but the boy fled, in case the vicar recognised him and told his father.

His father didn't want him to play with Gore.

'Why, Daddy?'

'That's why!'

It was through his friendship with Gore he met Tilly. Previously the nearest he got to her was watching her from a distance as she walked on Sunday afternoons up the village to the Methodist chapel. He could never decide whether she was better looking than his mother. She wore blue or white sleeveless frocks and long white gloves which came up nearly to her elbows. It was said she had a different hat for every month of the year. All of them had clusters of wax fruit or finch feathers. If it rained she wore a belted mackintosh. His mother's rain-coat was old, dull, had one button missing and one hanging and her legs were vein knots pulsing through thick stockings.

Tilly's feet were arched, curved. Like tongues. Her face, his mother's face and the face on the Blessed Virgin's statue in his father's room, were the best-looking faces in Butlershill. But his mother's eyes and the Virgin's eyes were soft. Tilly's were savage. When she walked to the

Methodist chapel she looked like a beautiful hawk, the Bible clutched in her hand like dead meat. The boy knew she had fierce religion.

Her husband, Bobby, was smaller than her and had to walk with short quick steps to keep up with her. He had a head like a saucepan – round, face flat; the tiny eyes, nose, mouth, looking as if they had been faintly sketched on with red crayon. For a moustache he had a thin line of blond stubble which looked like the bristle on bacon rind.

'God help him but he's got a face in need of a miracle,' the boy had heard his mother say. 'What she ever saw in him I'll never know.'

'She saw his bank book,' replied his father. 'She didn't come down from the North to marry a pauper, that's one sure thing.'

'Well, he's a cheerful soul, that's the main thing. All he lives for is his religion.'

'Get away outa that! When he's selling his insurance he's the buck would clean your clock for you. Religion, me foot! Apart from hating the Pope, what do they believe in?'

'I know, Daddy, Gore told me. They believe . . .'

'I told you I didn't want you playing with that fellah all the time.'

'Why, Daddy?'

'Never mind why!'

He was going to argue but he looked at his father's fists. They were the size of mallets.

One afternoon his father had caught them in the

creamery lavatory. They had gone in because Gore wanted to mickey measure. The creamery was beside the barracks. The local farmers brought their milk to it. At the back, perched on a few boards over a small river, was a lavatory with galvanised sides and a wooden door. In the door was an eye-hole, so the creamery manager could, as he crouched, keep watch.

Apart from the graveyard it was Gore's favourite haunt. He had followed him in and, his buttons undone, stood looking at Gore removing his pants. He decided to peep out the eye-hole. To his horror he saw his father coming across the ploughed field towards them. He had spotted them going in. The boy could tell from the fierce look on his face, he suspected what was going on. His great boots thick with clay, his fists swinging, he pounded towards them determined to catch them in the act.

Such was his dumb panic he couldn't warn Gore. He however had sensed catastrophe and when his father burst in on top of them, somehow had his pants back up though his braces were in a hopeless tangle.

'What the hell dirty work's going on here?'

His fist was in the air, ready to strike.

He knew if his father hit him he'd hate him for the rest of his days.

Desperate to avoid that, he somehow dredged up a lifebelt of a lie.

'All me money, Daddy, it's fallen down the hole. There's loads of pennies down there, we're only trying to get it back. Can you help us, Daddy?'

Instinctively, like a cat, he had landed on his feet. Nothing concerned his father more than money. A penny lost was a disaster. The boy remembered an evening when the whole house was turned upside down for a halfpenny that escaped through a hole in his pocket.

Immediately his father's fury vanished to be replaced by miserly concern as he peered through the lavatory seat into the murky waters below.

'Cripes, we might have to make a dam!'

He sent them to the tool shed for wellingtons, shovels and the riddle. When they returned he was sitting on the lavatory, boots off, sleeves rolled up, his face determined, excited. The more awkward the task, the better he liked it.

'Are we going to build a dam, Daddy?'

'No. We'll do the gold prospector on it – we'll riddle it out.'

They followed him down into the river. The lavatory was directly above their heads. The water ran black, the mud on the bed deep. The boy held the riddle and just as his father shovelled the first slap of muck into it they heard the lavatory door clap shut. They looked up. Nothing. Then to their amazement, they saw, hanging above them like a full moon, the creamery manager's naked posterior.

'Hold on there, hold on there!' his father shouted.

'What? What?'

Now the bearded face of the manager appeared to them.

'You'll have to wait. Some money's dropped down here. We're searching for it.'

'You can search or shift, Sergeant. But Nature must take its course.'

They had to move up river. His father had a sneer of disgust and contempt on his lips.

'You've landed us right in it, me buck.'

The waste pipe from the creamery stuck out from the river bank. It began to dribble, then discharge a full flow of hot water, skim and grease. Swirling like smoke through the black water, within seconds it had the river turned a foul milky, medicine grey.

'Cripes. It's purulent!'

His father gave up. He clambered out after him, then helped drag Gore out, who was sweating with worry, his eyes darting like a frightened animal. They were saved. But for days he had to keep away from Gore.

In the front, above the noise of the engine, they could hear Bobby and Tilly arguing. The van increased in speed as their voices rose in anger.

'You can't worship God and Mammon, Tilly.'

'You ought to know. You're the one with the purse strings.'

In the half-light he thought he saw a stain of blood on his trousers. He moved towards the windows to get a better look. It was only a bit of dirt from the demesne wall.

It annoyed him that he couldn't blame anyone but himself for the mess he was in. It had something to do with Gore, his father's fist and Tilly but he was the one on his way to Bundoran where, whatever the outcome, he would betray his religion and his country.

Gore was crawling round the van, thumbing his nose, giggling, trying to make him laugh.

'Sssh. They'll hear us.'

'Sure they'll have to find us sooner or later.'

For Gore it was just a madcap day out. But he was the one with the Sacred Host in his pocket and terrifying thoughts in his head. Gore was picking at his teeth with a straw, grinning at him, his eyes hunting. His head was clipped up to the top of his ears but the crown was thick with hair, so that it looked as if his scalp was divided by an encircling fringe. He was funny but troubling.

The first time they met up after the creamery lavatory incident they had gone to the quarry, climbing right to the top, from where they threw stones down hoping to start an avalanche of rock. When they didn't succeed they lay in the long grass smoking rolled strips of newspaper. On one of the strips was a photograph of the Pope. Gore had definite views on Catholicism.

'The Pope's married to a secret nun. Whiskey is the Devil's broth. And the bit of bread RCs get on their tongues at Mass is all me eye! How could it be the body of Christ? If that was so, if you stuck a knife in it, it'd bleed. Wouldn't it?'

The boy knew the Pope wasn't married to anyone. That was the whole point. If he was he'd be just the same as any other leader. And since wine became the blood of Christ, surely whiskey couldn't be all that bad?

Only Gore's point about the Host worried him. Because he'd often thought the same thing himself. Unlike Gore, though, he'd never dream of saying it aloud. He'd heard the priest say in a sermon, that if any boy or girl stuck a knife in the sacred Bread of Life, it would so bleed that the stabber would drown in a rising tide of blood and, run to escape as fast as they might, nothing could save them from terrible death.

In bed at night he tortured himself with stabbing night-mares of pursuing blood, the knife in his hand becoming heavier and heavier, until it finally dragged him to a stop, anchoring him to the ground and so allowing the chasing red tide to lick up his legs, surge through his pockets, seep into his mouth until his useless tongue could no longer cry for mercy and forgiveness.

The thought of stabbing the Host frightened him more than his father's fists. It also intrigued him. He couldn't stop himself playing with the idea. He knew that tempting himself with evil plots was almost as bad as the act itself but he couldn't help it. Especially when Gore was around.

'Why don't you get it on Sunday and we'll meet in the wood and I'll have me penknife?' '

'No. I'd be caught.'

'Cowardy custard wouldn't touch mustard.'

'If I died I'd go to Hell and burn for ever.'

'Not if your name's not written down.'

'Is that what Methodists believe?'

'It's what me sister told me. She knows the Bible by heart. Her and Uncle Bobby have their own religion.'

'What is it?'

'The Church of the Holy Word Truth Spreaders. Only the Bible knows. And you have to wash at sun up and sun down. And you're not allowed sweets except on Sundays.'

'How many people in their religion?'

'Two. Me sister and Uncle Bobby. But it's not numbers, it's the Word that counts.'

That was the great thing about being a Protestant. They could believe anything they wanted. No one told them what to think. You were your own Pope, like Bobby and Tilly, and it wouldn't cost you a thought sticking the Host with a penknife.

But no matter how tempted, he knew he would never actually steal the Host. He walked and slept balanced by fears. Nothing weighed heavy enough in the scales of his soul to make him do it. His life was poised between adventure and safety. Between his mother and father. Between love and loneliness. Only one thing could tip him over the edge. His father's fist. Fist. Raw fingers, gristle, bone, blood. When he looked at his pale face in the mirror he knew he would smash like a cup.

Shooting up what must have been a hump-backed bridge over a railway line or canal, they seemed to lurch through space, then down with a bump that heaved his stomach to his mouth and clattered his body up and down on the floor of the van. He was sure they were going to crash. It would be God's vengeance. In his pocket he felt the bulge of his handkerchief and thought he could feel the Host swelling and pulsing against his thigh. In the front Tilly and Bobby were now singing a hymn.

> Oh light the flame, Lord
> Oh keep it burning
> My heart is yearning
> For eternal love . . .

Tilly's voice was high and shrill, Bobby's a low nasal whine; but somehow, together they made music. On their way to spread the True Word to the Papists of Bundoran they were rehearsing courage and righteousness.

Gore's eyes were resting on him.

'Will we measure our mickeys?'

'No.'

'Why?'

'That's why.'

He wasn't going to measure his mickey in the back of a van walloping along the Fermanagh roads and him with the Body of Jesus in his pocket. He prayed to the Blessed Virgin, promising her he'd never do it again if she somehow delivered him from the mess he was in and brought him safely home.

His mother would be going crazy looking for him. She'd have his dinner on a plate covered with a saucepan lid, warming on top of the range. She'd send his father out the back to search for him. Out by the buckled heap of galvanised sheets and charred rafters from the sheds.

It was he who set them alight. No one knew. Not his mother, not Tilly, not even Gore. His heart was slowly filling with black secrets. If his father ever found out he'd skin him alive with his leather belt.

He lay in the van, his father's fists swirling in his head. He was heaping live coals on them, trying to burn them in revenge. It was because of those fists he had started the fire. He the Sergeant's son setting fire to half the barracks! Your mother's slaps didn't count. When she hit him there was gentleness in her hands. Like she was plumping a cushion.

Gore went to the rear windows and looked out.

'Loch Erne,' he whispered.

The vast stretch of water spread like a grey police blanket over the countryside. Four swans flew straight as a spear just above it, then skidded to a rest, sitting still as ornaments on a mantelpiece.

'It's the biggest lake in Europe.'

'No it's not. The Caspian Sea is.'

His father drilled river lengths and mountain heights into him. And capital cities of the world.

'It friggin' isn't. That's salty water.'

'Oh, do you mean freshwater?'

'You know well I do. Loch Erne divides Fermanagh in two.'

'Lough Neagh is twice the size. And there's a lake in Russia even bigger.'

'What's the name of it?'

'I've forgotten for the moment.'

Gore snorted and threw himself down on the straw in a sulk. Ignoring his mood, knowing it wouldn't last very long, he carried on looking out.

'It's certainly the biggest lake in Fermanagh, I'll admit that.'

The straw smelt musty and he shifted his position when he felt with his knee a sticky mess of broken eggs.

Every time the van went round a twisty bend, it tilted to one side as if the springs were gone and a grating noise came from the engine.

'Mind you, by the shape of it, I don't think it's a lake at all. It's a river pretending to be one.'

Between two clumps of distant trees a spill of sunlight poured down a hill and turned the waters blue, the swans to gold.

If only he were a swan. But swan's blood is cold blood. They would never be able to feel the hot flesh of Tilly Roberts's thigh.

They drove by what looked like an Army hut. It was roofed with corrugated sheets, painted a gun-metal grey and over the windows were wire grilles. Standing by the entrance were about twenty young men, all dressed in dark-blue suits. The books they clutched the boy knew were Bibles. They were having a chat before going inside to pray. Bobby Roberts beeped the horn at them in a passing greeting.

The men in their sharp suits and cropped hair looked severe. Religion in the North had a sword in it. In Butlershill they had the sword too but they also had vestments, candles, flowers, holy water, bells and the almost visible tang of incense. And Sunday was a sporting day.

In the North his father told him you couldn't fart on

the Sabbath without written permission from the head of the Orange Order.

'Oh that's a fact!'

They left the little church far behind but it still travelled with the boy, the men like a painting frozen in his mind along with the swans on the lake.

He lay down in the straw. Feelings burnt. Flesh burned you. Bone. Fist. Thigh softness. Sacred wafer. They entered your brain and set your head alight. Fleshy thoughts once in behind your eyes made you afraid to look too long at people in case they caught fire.

'Look at me when I'm talking to you.'

'Talk to him, not at him and he'll look at you.'

'No one's talking to you. Shifty eyes and bitten fingernails proclaim criminality. They're two cast-iron signs. It's a well-known fact.'

'I don't bite my nails, Daddy.'

'Show me.'

Why hadn't he kept his mouth shut? Everybody knew he bit his nails. His thumbnails were his favourites. For some mad reason he had walked himself right to the brink. As if inviting his father to push him over. Burning the shed, going into Tilly's bedroom, stealing the Host, flaming thoughts – they hadn't happened then. Already though, in his mind, he must have been playing with fire.

'I said show me!'

He held his fingers out. The nails were bitten to the quicks. His father's face curdled with disgust. He gripped each one in turn, pulling, pressing, staring at them like they were bits of rotting wood.

'Look. Look. Bitten. Look. Have you seen this?'

His mother was always dragged into his rages.

'It's nothing to do with me. Leave him alone, can't you? I've told him not to.'

His father's fingers were vices, twisting, tightening, paining. And more and more his mother was unable to protect him.

'Leave me alone, leave me alone,' he screamed. 'Let me go, let me go.'

And then for some reason he decided to bring Gore Kemp into it.

'Gore Kemp bites his nails and he doesn't get touched.'

His father's blow seemed to light the kitchen up and like lightning in the sky it couldn't be stopped. His fist glinted like the sun on a raised axe. He smashed like a cup. The surprise and quickness of the explosion was half the pain. He remembered shattering back against the dresser, then hitting the floor. His mind divided in a glaze of stars. Away on the edge of space he heard his mother cry. He was still lying limp as his enraged father dipped his fingers in a saucer of iodine. He was vaguely aware of him pressing his fingers into the saucer, rolling them in the iodine like he was taking fingerprints. He came to in his mother's arms but struggled away from her. He wanted to be alone. In a dark corner where he could balance the pain and the shame. He would hate his father forever and a day now.

Dazed he walked round to the back of the barracks. He'd lie down in one of the sheds. Going through the hen pen he slipped and lay on the ground too sorry for himself to bother getting up. The hens, at first frightened away, came towards him and stood giving him gawking sideways looks.

Making for the potato shed he met Guard Magee coming out of the oil house carrying the paraffin can. He stunk of tobacco and Guinness and was singing and laughing to himself, though on duty, obviously drunk. He staggered away leaving the oil-house door unlocked.

The boy went in and sat with the door half open to give himself some light. The spanner was still attached to the valve tap and hadn't been turned off properly. Oil was splashing from the barrel on to the concrete floor.

Already it had begun to flow out the door and down the concrete path alongside the rest of the sheds. Oil was colder than water – 'til you put a match to it. He was warmer than blood but a fist had made him ice. It wasn't the pain of the blow that hurt most. It was the shame and sadness that his father had made him at a stroke the same as any of the other beaten boys in the village. He felt lonely. Like he was dead. He needed heat. He knew that next door in the police lavatory was a candle in a blue enamelled holder and on the tray a box of matches. On the back of the lavatory door, stuck on a four-inch nail, was a wad of quartered newspaper pages. He got the matches and a sheet of the paper and went back into the oil house.

The oil hitting the concrete splashed like handclapping. It slicked out the door in jagged rainbow rings.

His father whom he loved had hit him and bruised his

heart. The inside of his head was black with pain. Love couldn't be beaten in but it could be beaten out.

He tore the piece of newspaper in two and rolled one of the strips into a cigarette. Gore had shown him how. He lit the end of the roll, stared at the flame, then blew it out. The end glowing he pulled the smoke into his mouth. The strong taste of it coated the back of his throat.

On the floor under the barrel was a cloth for wiping accidental spills. He stared at it for a long time then lit the end of it. He threw it back down and watched it smoulder. Like a moth, the dull fire nibbled through it.

He began to cry. Tears couldn't quench the shame he felt. He was a good boy. He only wanted to be happy.

He wandered back through the hen pen and up the path on the married quarters' side of the barracks. Tiptoeing in the hall door he went to his room and on top of the iron bed cried himself to sleep.

In the front of the van the Robertses were singing 'Fare thee well Enniskillen, fare thee well for a while . . .' Their voices sounded sweeter than when they sang the hymn.

Gore went quickly to the rear windows.

'Quick,' he whispered, 'we're going through my town. See yonder – that's Portora, my school. See down there – that's the military barracks.'

The boy saw a Catholic church and directly opposite a Protestant one. Enniskillen was where Gore lived except when on holiday in Butlershill.

'That's Blake's pub. That's where me da gets mildewed

drunk. See that big pillar – that's the Cole monument. The town's on an island, you know!'

Gore's small pale face was pressed to the glass.

'Maybe they'll stop for a cup of tea.'

'They never stop anywhere 'til they get there.'

His face a saucer of sadness he lay down on the straw, the boy beside him.

'Do you ever get beaten, Gore? By your father?'

'He doesn't beat me. He kicks me. I was in hospital once for a week. They told them I fell off the wall.'

In the front the singing stopped and they lay on the straw listening to the van roar its way up a hill. Slowly it groaned to the top and when coasting down the other side Bobby began to preach.

'Cold water, hot water, spring water, tap water, holy water, Boyne water – none of it washes with the Lord. Ironworks, roadworks, goodworks – they'll not save you if your name's not written down on high. Hope, rope, soap, the Pope – none of them can wash you clean unless Jesus has washed you in the blood of Calvary . . .'

The van swerved dangerously up on to the grass verge, tumbling the two boys in a heap to one side and back to the centre again when the van righted itself.

Tilly Roberts screamed

'Watch where you're going, you cretin! Have you gone blind as well as stupid?'

'Sorry, sorry. The wheel bucked outa me hands!'

In the back they could hear her derisive snort and feel the hostile silence between them throbbing like a part of the engine. Then they heard a slap and Bobby's squealing temper.

'Cut it out now, I'm warning you, you bitch.'

The boy knew religion didn't stop fights. His mother and father often rowed, knelt to say the Rosary and started fighting again as soon as they stood up from praying. Men and women fought because it seemed they had to.

Gore was trying to be funny by stuffing straw down his trousers, socks, inside his shirt and up his sleeves. He looked bloated and unreal. A grinning boy scarecrow flying over the fields and roads.

When he laughed at him, Gore was pleased. He liked to play the comic. He found it hard to sit still.

'Let's see it.'

Kneeling, the boy took the handkerchief from his pocket and gently unfolded the Host. They stared at it. Gore took out his penknife.

'Let's do it now. Come on.'

'Not on your life.'

'It'll be all right. The straw will mop up the blood if it bleeds.'

'No. We'll do it by the seaside.'

'Can I touch it?' He reached out a finger.

'It feels like a bit of wafer.'

'That's what it is.'

'I thought you said it was Christ's Body?'

'It is. But during Mass it becomes Christ. It's called transubstantiation. It's a miracle.'

'If it really does bleed I'll give you all the money I have. I promise.'

'If it bleeds,' the boy whispered, 'we'll be dead men.'

*

When the priest placed it on his dry tongue he closed his lips but held it away from the roof of his mouth in case it got wet. Hands joined in a display of piety he walked down the aisle and into the pew beside his mother. Bowing his head as if praying, he slid his hands over his face and somehow got the Host off his tongue and into his left fist. He felt every eye in the church on the back of his head. Perspiration dripped down his forehead. He was sure all the statues of all the saints were staring at him. When he peeped through his fingers he saw Jesus in one of the Stations of the Cross looking directly at him. He thought of his father hitting him and he thought of Tilly Roberts. He put his fist into his pocket.

After Mass he made for the demesne where Gore was waiting for him. As he ran along the road he prayed his pocket wouldn't explode. He began to think that if only there was water near he could somehow escape if it started bleeding.

Gore was waiting in behind the demesne wall, his knife in his hand and a big flat stone on the ground in front of him.

'We won't do it here. We'll go to the lake. That way the blood, if it comes, will get mixed up in water and we can escape.'

Gore dismissed his fears but when the Host was placed on the stone and he raised his knife, the boy saw his darting eyes narrow with worry.

'Right enough we'd be trapped here, if it bled, which it won't. I know. Tilly and Uncle Bobby go to the seaside every Sunday, to preach. We could stow away in the back of the van and do it at Bundoran. It's the Atlantic Ocean there. The blood of all Heaven and Hell couldn't drown that. What do you think? And we'll get slab toffee there, it's great.'

There was a reason for everything. He knew why he had started the fire in the oil house but he couldn't work out exactly why he had stolen the Host. What had given him the mad courage? It was the crime of the century. What force or powerful magic had soaked his brain?

Tilly was still angry with Bobby, her fury spreading beyond criticism of his driving. Gore couldn't bear to listen and blocking his ears burrowed his head under the straw.

'Drive? You couldn't drive a nail! Lord why have you inflicted this second death on me? Married to the meanest miser among men. Drive me mad, yes! You had the thorns and nails, Lord, and I have the biggest Roman of them all sitting here beside me. A right wee cup of vinegar!'

'That's enough now, Tilly. A house divided! If we don't pull together we'll smash on the rocks. You hadn't a rag to wipe a snotter 'til I come. If you don't like it you can get out now. Do you want me to stop, do you?'

Tilly stopped shouting. The van drove on.

Bobby Roberts was the first person on the scene of the fire. He'd been driving past the barracks when he saw smoke billowing up from the sheds. When he ran into the day-room to raise the alarm, Guard Magee was slumped in a chair drunk. He then ran round to the kitchen but only the boy's mother was there, his father having gone out on patrol. Her caterwauling however attracted half the village and soon the back of the barracks was a mayhem of bodies pitching buckets of water up on the shed roof. The boy awoken by the commotion knew immediately what was happening. He calmly walked round and from the hen pen watched the blaze. He felt detached, his head cool, his thoughts bitter. His father had no right to hit him.

Bobby Roberts was in a fit of panic, his face red with mad useless energy. One bucket of water he threw hit Guard Magee full in the face.

'Christ,' laughed Magee, 'you'd be a great man to have in Hell.'

The water was carrying the burning oil down the path towards the hen house. Many of the men were chortling at the good of it all. Were the barracks to burn down it would be a day for the history books.

He began to shiver as the enormity of what was happening penetrated his soul. A fierce anger quickly built up in him at the confraternity of fools throwing water on burning oil.

He raced to the tool shed, grabbed two shovels, then ran back round to the fire. He began to shovel clay from the garden on to the river of fire. Somebody grabbed the other shovel and soon all the men were throwing handfuls of clay on the flames. Within minutes the fire was out.

The boy could see his mother looking out from a window. She was crying and had a rosary beads working through her fingers.

Then his father, his eyes gigantic with shock, arrived.

'The young fellah saved the day, Sergeant. He's a great gauson altogether.'

When everyone had at last gone home, his father took him in his arms and kissed him.

'You're the best boy in Ireland. What would we do without you?'

He was a criminal for biting his fingernails. He was a hero for putting out a fire which he himself had started. Life was a sham, his own emotions mocking him. Why the fire broke out no one was able to discover. It was a mystery. Some things couldn't be explained. Like transubstantiation. Even a kiss was two-faced.

He was happy lying in the van with Gore. No one could touch him. Only his thoughts. Closing his eyes he pretended he was an aeroplane.

'Gore – I'm an aeroplane.'

'I'm a submarine.'

Only for Gore he wouldn't have met Tilly. He wished he was in the front sitting beside her. She wore perfume behind her ears and under her chin. He wondered was she wearing her garter. Gore didn't know he had been in her room. No one knew. Except her. She had something to do with him stealing the Host but he couldn't as yet grasp exactly what it was.

He had been in her house, playing with Gore. They had gone upstairs and were jumping up and down on his bed. They decided to play hide-and-seek and Gore went outside into the yard and told him to stay in the bedroom for sixty seconds and then to come and look for him.

He counted sixty and when he came out on the landing Tilly from her bedroom was looking out at him. He stopped and looked at her. Her eyes were big and firm.

'Come here.'

The landing was carpeted. He hadn't walked on any before.

'Close the door.'

It closed with a gentle click. The bed was brass covered with a big fluffy eiderdown. The furniture was polished oak. Over the washstand hung a picture of the Queen.

'Do you pray? Do you?'

He wasn't sure whether she was stern or smiling.

'I pray at night and first thing in the morning.' He smiled at her. She tipped a small rectangular bottle on to her index finger, then dabbed behind her ears. She was known for her edgy temper but he wasn't scared. She jabbed the bottle down on the dressing table and turned and looked at him. Her eyes were dreamy brown.

'Snap my garter, boy. Snap my garter for the Lord.'

He giggled but she was deadly serious. Her hair was still back behind one of her ears. She held her wrap-around skirt open, revealing her right leg. Above the top of her stocking was naked flesh. Her leg ran smooth as mercury into her high-heel shoe. He went on one knee in front of her, frightened, a nervous smile on his lips. Where the suspender clasped the stocking he hooked his finger in.

'That's not my garter.'

He then saw a frilly black band trimmed with lace further down her leg. He hadn't seen a garter like this before. His own were thin bands of elastic, the ends sewn together by his mother with white thread.

He knew he was blushing as he took the garter in his fingers and snapped it against her thigh. Plack!

'Off you go now and play with Gore.'

Her face was pale as snow and firm as ice. He ran from the room in a daze, his finger burning from the touch of flesh. He looked at it expecting to see a blister.

Why had she asked him to do that? And what had garters to do with the Lord? He could hear Gore out in the yard, calling. Ignoring him he went out the front door and made for the hayshed at the back of Reilly's pub. The hay was soft, warm and dreamy. Since being forced to sleep on his own, hay was the nearest he got to the sweet feeling of his mother's body. He often lay alone in Reilly's shed.

When he hooked his finger in Tilly's suspender her leg quivered. Like a horse trembling her skin against flies. Or water shivering against wind. He kissed his finger, reached down inside his trousers, curled up and let thoughts of his mother, father, Tilly dance in his mind like flames.

Next day he told Gore he'd steal the Host.

The van slammed to an abrupt stop. Bobby Roberts shouted something and a man with an English accent shouted back.

'No, go ahead, you're OK, mate!'

Scrambling to the windows they saw a stationary British Army lorry, the driver lazing over the steering wheel and a soldier out on the road leaning across the bonnet, his rifle in the aim position.

They were still in the North. The soldier's eyes followed them all the way to the next corner.

He tried to understand why countries were divided but couldn't at all understand why men and women were. If he were Bobby Roberts he wouldn't be at odds with Tilly. Women wanted praise, comfort and their garter snapping, simple as that. Love. All his mother wanted was peace of mind and to laugh. Instead she spent more and more time crying. When his father saw her tears spurt it infuriated him.

'Cripes but your bladder is very near your eye.'

Gore crawled to him and whispered, 'Does your father arrest anyone?'

'Not as often as he'd like.'

'Who does he arrest?'

'Tinkers. Drunks. But he lets them out again. He's hoping for a murderer all the time.'

'Does he ever get a hold of any smugglers?'

'No. But he knows who they are.'

Gore's eyes blinked but his expression gave nothing away.

Bobby Roberts was a preacher, an insurance man, the egg man and the boy knew he was also a smuggler. That's why Gore was quizzing him. The very van they were travelling in was used chiefly for carrying goods over and back across the Border. Razor blades, furniture, eggs, lengths of steel, cigarettes, butter, hens, farm animals – anything that could be bought cheap on one side and sold dear on the other.

'How does he know who the smugglers are?'

'He sees them. Even in the dark.'

'Who are they?'

'You ought to know, Gore.'

Gore blinked and blinked and scowled

'I'll give you a crack on the gob if you're saying Uncle Bobby is one.'

'I never mentioned him. If he is one it's nothing to do with me. He can smuggle all he wants for all I care.'

'Well, he only smuggles eggs. That's all. To help old ladies who can't afford them.'

'Oh, so he is a smuggler?'

Gore was furious. He launched himself at the boy, trying to hit him. They rolled over and over wrestling for supremacy.

'Quit it. They'll hear us.'

'So what?'

'You're squashing the Host in me pocket.'

'Don't care about it or you.'

They broke free from one another and lay panting. Gore crawled into a corner of the van and sat sulking. The straw still stuffed inside his clothes inflated his body, making his head look even smaller than usual. In a mood he always looked funny, odd, but his moods never lasted long. Forgetting quickly he forgave easily. It was lovely having a friend like that.

The boy knew about moods. His father's sometimes

lasted for weeks. The dull scowl on his father's grey face bled into every nook and cranny of the house, killing his mother's spirit and squashing the boy's soul. His moods soaked even into your hair and clothes and stunk of rotten potatoes. Moods were the soul's smelly breath. Its voice was silent crying.

'What else do you know about Uncle Bobby?'

'What you don't know won't hurt you, Gore.'

'I hate you.'

Bobby Roberts was a smuggler but the boy knew something else about him. Twice a week he crossed into the Six Counties where he was a member of a part-time militia set up by the Belfast government to defend themselves against the IRA. They were given rifles, carried out night-time patrols and were paid.

'Oh yes,' he heard his father say to Guard Magee, 'lives down here but crosses over for the Queen's shilling. The best of both worlds. The educated blaggard. It's a goldmine to them, that Border. A veritable goldmine to him and his ilk.'

He wondered how on earth anyone could entrust Bobby with a rifle, his eyesight being so poor. He wore glasses and put another pair on top of them whenever he had to read. He was so short-sighted, when people saw his van approach they stood up on the grassy verge until he passed.

'Nothing wrong with his peepers when it comes to counting money, let me tell you.'

'Oh leave him alone,' the boy's mother said. 'He's a Protestant, so if there's money going to defend them, why shouldn't he get it same as the rest of them? Bobby doesn't believe half of it anyway. She's the one swallows it, though, hook, line and sinker. She's pure poison if ever I saw it.'

His mother didn't like Tilly. She didn't like women if they had opinions of their own and were good-looking as well. She always wanted to be the centre of attention. He often sat with her in a neighbour's house, the room full of women, all listening to her and laughing at her humour, most of which was aimed at men.

'It's not only their dinner they want. If they were the ones got pregnant, the midnight knock on the door wouldn't happen so often.'

Her remarks were always followed by an avalanche of laughter. She loved being loved. Surrounded by the humbler village women she was a queen bee in a happy hive.

Whenever she met Tilly Roberts, though, they smiled icicles at each other. Tilly had her own views, her own hive. His mother couldn't stand her.

What would she say if she found out that he had been in Tilly's bedroom, had gone on his knee before her and hooked his finger in her suspender? That his body bubbled every time he thought of it? He would die if she ever found out.

He himself was a smuggler but much worse than Bobby Roberts. Bobby smuggled for money but he smuggled for revenge. There was nothing meaner, cheaper than revenge. He didn't own a van but in his head he carried flesh, fire and in his pocket the Sacred Body of Christ who died on the cross to save the world.

The Eucharist was the cornerstone of his religion. Each time Mass was celebrated the small round white wafer became Jesus. And when you took it on your tongue and swallowed it you were partaking in the miracle of miracles. Yet here he was smuggling it, in his father's white handkerchief, out of the Republic into the North and back to the Republic again miles and miles away from where anyone would know him. He was certain no other boy in Ireland ever did what he was going to do with it. He was going to stick a knife in it to . . . He tried to banish the mad thoughts from his head.

'Let's be bicycles, Gore.'

Lying on their backs, legs raised, feet touching sole to sole, they began pedalling.

'In Bundoran you get great ice cream cones. And slab toffee dead cheap. And there's chair-o'-planes there as well and rocking horses.'

Gore didn't care. He was only looking forward to a good time.

He couldn't work out which was your country – the heart or the brain. They seemed foreign to each other. But either way your parents were among the people who stood on the border in between. Thoughts had to be smuggled. A fist could easily mash them into chaos.

'There's a great swimming pool on the edge of the sea.'

'We haven't togs.'

'We can skinny dip. No one cares in Bundoran. And there's great rocks to climb. When you get to the top on a clear day you can see America.'

Gore's face shone with joy and promise.

They felt the van slowing and the engine rev up before being switched off.

They heard footsteps, then men's voices.

'Where are you headin'?'

'Bundoran.'

'Where have you come from?'

'Butlershill in the County Cavan.'

'What have you got in the van?'

'Nothing. Only a harmonium. We're preachers.'

'Open up.'

The van was going to be searched. They dived under the straw, the boy's heart pounding. Feet shuffled round to the back and the doors wrenched open.

'What's that?'

'That's the harmonium.'

'What's the straw for?'

'For eggs. I sell eggs. As well as insurance.' Bobby's voice was high-pitched with nerves.

'Do you carry animals? I smell pigs.'

'No, no, oh no. There's only ever been the odd hen in it.'

'How odd?' There was a snigger, then a silence in which the boy could hear Tilly humming a hymn on the other side of the partition.

It was stuffy under the straw. It had a musty, stale whiff. If whoever they were didn't go soon, he'd have to come up for air.

The van sagged. One of them had stepped into the back. There was a swishing sound as he swept the straw with his foot, searching it.

Gore was the first to be discovered, the man standing on him, causing him to cry out in pain.

'Agh, me friggin' foot!'

The boy spluttering up from the straw saw a Customs officer, gigantic in the confines of the van, staring down at him. Another officer peered in from the roadway.

What if he was searched and they discovered the Host? Was it illegal to smuggle Jesus across the Border? He gulped at the fresh air coming in the open doors.

The Customs men were looking at Bobby, awaiting explanation. His face twitched in utter shock. A nervous froth of spit sat on his lower lip.

'I . . . what are youse doing here? They're not supposed to be here at all. That's God's truth. Tilly! That's me wife's young brother. And that lad's the Sergeant's son in Butlershill. Tilly! They must have hid before we driv away. Tilly! I . . . I . . . Tilly!'

The uniformed men looked at Bobby, the boys and at Tilly when she came round to see what the commotion was, as if they and the straw-filled van had landed from another planet.

The sun shone in along the gap where the door was hinged to the side. Dust swimming in its angled beam burnished the straw to brilliant gold.

The officers were tall and heavy, one of them with a big belly straining to get out past his buttons. The buttons on their tunics were the same colour as the golden straw.

Tilly looked fierce. The boy had never seen her in such severe clothes. She wore a black hat with a peak and a red band, a black jacket, black tight skirt, black stockings and shoes and black nylon see-through gloves. Her eyes raged with fiery annoyance.

'Come here to me.'

Gore crawling to her, she reached in and lugged him on to the road. Holding him with one hand she slapped him about the face with the other. He squirmed and squealed, wriggled down on to the road and rolled for safety right in under the van.

'They stowed away without telling us,' Bobby muttered, as if trying to excuse his wife's ferocious display.

The Customs men exchanged looks and got in to their car parked alongside. The boy got out of the van and stood before Tilly. She looked at him long and hard. Her hair was up under her pillbox hat.

'Go on, beat him as well as me,' Gore shouted from under the van.

'He's not mine to beat.' Her accent was clipped, sharp, cold.

Smiling he looked from her hard gaze towards a bombed-out building some distance back down the road. A British Customs Post bombed by the IRA. The men who stopped them were Irish Customs, so they were out of the North and now in Donegal.

Bobby grabbing Gore's ankle yanked him out to his feet. Thinking he was going to get another welting he began to blab their reason for wanting to come to Bundoran.

'He's got a Communion Host in his pocket. He stole

it from Mass this morning. We're going to stick a knife in it to see will she bleed. If it does, the sea will wash it all away.'

The boy was shocked, shattered. Tilly Roberts held out her hand. Bobby stood, his face gawping, not believing what he was hearing. The Customs men watched from their car.

He didn't want to give the Host to her. She was an enemy of his religion, probably his country as well. Already there was a gloating look on her face. There was no knowing what she would do with it. Her hand was still outstretched. How could he hand it over to her? His mother had called her pure poison. It would be like handing Christ to the Devil. He moved from foot to foot and whimpered, trying to make himself cry. Maybe sobs would save him. He was going to murder Gore Kemp when he got the chance. Gore already ashamed wouldn't look him in the eye. Bobby stared at Tilly, trying to understand her. The boy hated her now. And her garter. She stood without moving a muscle, staring into his guts with her lovely hard eyes.

'Give.'

He could feel the Host jump in his pocket. It felt sweaty as if full of blood, throbbing in sorrow for the worst crime a boy could commit. He stood along the Border, alone, lost, ready to weep bitter tears. It was the faith of all traitors.

'If you don't hand it over, I'll have to tell your father.'

She was the cruellest woman in the world.

'You tell on me, I'll tell on you.'

He was barely aware of the words slipping through his lips. He hated himself now. Not only was he a traitor, now he was a blackmailer. Like her. From the moment he had entered her bedroom he was doomed.

Bobby was looking at them, his head trembling in puzzlement.

Her eyes were slits of anger. Slowly her lips parted in a thin smile. He believed she was blushing. She spun round and, her high heels clicking on the country road, walked to the passenger door.

Across the blue sky a small, snarling aeroplane trailed a tail of letters spelling the slogan – 'DONNELLY'S SAUSAGES FOR YOU'.

Bundoran was creamy, yellow, blue and rock. The streets sandy, faces brown, golf course shiny green. Sitting outside a restaurant, Bobby and Tilly drinking tea, he and Gore licking huge ice cream cones squirted with raspberry juice, they watched the world go sauntering by.

He was surprised that from the moment they arrived in the town Bobby and Tilly were all smiles. They stepped from the van like they were two different people. He couldn't understand the change in them. For the few remaining miles of the journey he had heard above the engine roar, mutterings, urgent whisperings and a burst of laughter. His back turned angrily on Gore, he lay on the straw trying to overhear them but couldn't. If they were up to something he had no idea what it was. Perhaps they were making up for the battering Gore received. He was glad he hadn't handed the Host to

Tilly. His threat worked. She threatened him first. Yet he couldn't work out why it was all right to go into her room and touch her flesh, yet it wasn't all right to let her have the Host.

Gore was happily licking his cone but he was persecuted by his thoughts. The raspberry juice glistened over his ice cream like fresh blood. A beggar musician playing a piano accordion limped along the street, a white stick dangling from his wrist. As he neared them the boy could see that the white accordion was faded with age to a nicotine brown. The man's eyes were dead marbles in his head. A piece of paper stuck to the accordion read – 'Blind since birth.'

He stopped playing right in front of where they sat and limped towards them, his greasy cap held out. Bobby grimaced and grinned; Tilly critically examined him with her eyes for fraud. The beggar waited.

'Please, thank you. Please, thank you.'

Gore stood up and from his pocket took some coins which he dropped in the cap.

'God Almighty bless you and reward you.'

Gore's face beamed with pleasure at his own generosity. His eyes hunted their faces for reaction. The boy smiled at him, forgiving him for blabbing their secret. If you got beaten, you blabbed.

Fist. He got beaten, he burnt the sheds.

Playing, the musician limped away. Tilly, recognising the tune, looked at Bobby, the edges of her mouth twitching. It was 'Faith Of Our Fathers'. The boy's mother called it 'The National Anthem of our religion.'

Tilly and Bobby were exchanging barely concealed contempt. It riddled their faces and eyes. They were like two soldiers deep in enemy country, giving the game away despite themselves. Soldiers of Christ. Their Christ. Not his. His was in his pocket. Listening to every thought in his head even before he thought of it. If the New Testament were rewritten he could well be included. 'And so Pilate delivered Jesus to an Irish boy from Butlershill who with a penknife did turn Bundoran into Calvary.'

Soon he and Gore would have to act. He began to sicken with fear. The pit of his stomach boiled with loneliness. He licked his cone and bit his stumpy thumbnail.

They walked along the street, turned a corner and there below them was the Atlantic Ocean. He had never seen the sea before. He hadn't realised it was so noisy. Booming, whooshing, yapping. Like a skittish foal, it came frolicking towards them but tripped and sprawled across the beach. It begged to be played with. The waves came in like a horse's mouth, lips curdled back, showing its teeth. Gore's eyes were calm before it. He couldn't wait to start playing but Tilly wouldn't let them out of her sight. She made them stand with her on the beach, nearer to the road than the water. People sat on towels or newspapers. The women had removed only their cardigans, the men their jackets; their shirts unbuttoned revealing Vs of chest to the sun.

Bobby came across the sands from the parked van, carrying the harmonium. Resting it in position, he opened it and looked at Gore.

'Give's that penknife of yours for a second.'

They thought at first he wanted it in connection with the organ, but taking it from him he put it directly into his pocket.

Gore looked dismayed but the boy in a trance of relief and joy couldn't believe his luck. The knife was confiscated. The Host could not now be stabbed. The Robertses whatever their beliefs were not going to allow such a travesty of religion. His heart leaped and the pressure lifted from his brain. He sank in relief to his knees and had to restrain himself from joining his hands in prayer. Bundoran was a wonderful place. The sky was blue, the ocean merry, the seagulls flying angels. The Host was safe in his pocket. He'd go to Confession during the week, then swallow it when his soul was back in a state of grace and never again would he light fires, touch garters or even dream of sacrilegious stabbing.

The harmonium was the height of a sewing machine but narrower. Bobby stood at it, his foot working the treadle, his stiff fingers pressing the keys. For a small instrument it produced a clattering sound which boomed out over the heads of the people and swallowed the sound of the sea.

Heads turned. The Robertses looked like preachers and the music had a hurdy-gurdy sound unlike Catholic hymns. They were obviously outsiders. The boy noticed the men staring at Tilly. He was proud to be at her side. She gazed towards the horizon, her severe beauty haunting the wind. The sand powdered the suede toecaps of her shoes. Her insteps arched like cows' tongues in a butcher's window. Her breasts pushed her jacket away from her. A cloud of perfumed flowers clung round her. She was better looking than his mother. He wondered was she wearing the garter. He'd snap it for her any day. For her. For the Lord. For anyone. Yes and would he set fire to the barracks any day? The Host in his pocket, would he . . . ? Barely a few minutes after his fervent promises here he was ready to go the same road again. Why didn't Jesus, who after all was right there in his pocket, chase the Devil out of his head?

Tilly was looking down at him. Why? Staring at him. Now she was smiling. The warmest smile he had ever seen on her face. Her flesh and bones, her teeth, lashes, eyebrows, marshmallow lips, ears so dainty – they shone like lights at him. He was mesmerised. He could no longer hear Bobby playing or the sound of the sea. She touched his cheek and bent close to him.

'Good boy.'

The day was golden and he was the luckiest boy in the world. He was away from the police station and his poor struggling mother and his father's heavy boots on the lino and the cold grip of the iron bed in which he lay alone. He was beside Tilly, a woman more beautiful even than the statue of the Blessed Virgin in his father's room. And she was smiling to him. He would walk on broken glass for her, give her his soul. Love was the opposite of fist.

She held her hand out to him, her palm upwards. In a dreamy moment he was about to reach out and hold it, when he realised with a terrible shock what it was she wanted. She wanted the Host. He was ensnared. He couldn't dodge her eyes. There was nowhere to run to. Her smile persecuted him. Unable to refuse he handed her the Body of Jesus wrapped in his father's handkerchief.

His brain buzzed hopelessly. He felt like fainting from shame. Gore was winking at him. Bobby Roberts with his silly spotted bow tie, fat fingers and two sets of spectacles looked clownish. The beach faces stared unaware of what was happening to him.

He had given in. A walloping made Gore give in. But he fell to a sign of warmth. A smile. He wanted to roar out his anger. He was a stubborn calf. But the sight of an udder, the rattle of a bucket and he'd come running. She touched his cheek, smiled and that was enough.

Her smile was a warm rope; his mother's heat a blanket. He slept on his own in a room with an empty fireplace and wallpaper with a scum of musty green damp. No matter how many police greatcoats were piled on him he could never get warm. There was no heat like a woman's body. The heat from the burning sheds was only skin-deep. Tilly's flesh, his mother's flesh – they warmed the brain and heart as well as your feet and shoulders. The sun in the Donegal sky was only a glowing cinder. One day it would burn out. But his mother's love could never be extinguished. And his father and all the men could shovel clay or sand on Tilly Roberts until there was no sand left and she'd still rage like a volcano.

He knew it was a terrible sin even to think it but there was no heat in Jesus. The only fire was flesh.

He was still sick, though, at the thought of the Host in Tilly's hand. He felt certain she was going to reveal it in some way to the people. To denigrate it before their eyes.

The organ stopped and Tilly, her eyes shut and hands raised, began preaching in a sing-song hysterical tone.

'Yes I am so happy since the Lord came into my life. He is the way, the life, the word. You cannot live without the Lord. Allow the Lord to cleanse your heart. I am so happy since He entered in. Thank you, Jesus. In the Bible which is the only written evidence we have it clearly states . . .'

Her voice swooped up and down, hitting some words, dragging others out like they were elastic. ' . . . I am SOOO HAPPY . . .' ' . . . THANK YOU, JES-US . . .'

Her intensity was such, people couldn't look away. Her legs apart, her high heels staked in the sand, her arms raised, the white handkerchief in her hand, she looked a nightmare more beautiful than the sea.

Bobby, clutching his Bible, butted in at the end of every phrase. 'Amen, sister, Amen.'

Gore, as soon as he saw they were carried away, came round to the boy's side. 'Come on and we'll go for a paddle. I've got money for slab toffee.'

'She's got the Host but.'

'So what? Come on. They'll be preaching for friggin' hours.'

'I can't, Gore. I've got to stay.'

A couple sunbathing nearby got up and moved away, the man shouting to Tilly, 'Catch yourself on, darlin', and give our heads a rest.'

Tilly was completely unaware of any opposition to her sermon. When she finished, Bobby began to speak, on his face a sweet smile of utter reasonableness.

'I didn't come here today to upset, cause trouble, give offence or stop youse enjoying yourselves. But the summer is ending, the harvest nigh and we are not saved. When Christ died on the Cross, He opened up a whole new chapter. Someday He's going to close it. Religion is only Sunday for most people but the Gospel is seven days a week. Cold water, hot water, holy water, Boyne water – it's not going to get you to Heaven. If your name's not written down, hope, rope, dope, the Pope – none of them can save you. I can't save you. Miracles can't save you. Only Jesus saves.'

The sunbathers tolerated Tilly but the boy could see they were hostile to Bobby. His smug smile and bow tie were annoying and so was the way he preached: as if it was obvious that what he was saying was so true only fools like his listeners could doubt it.

'You see vestments, incense, bells, candles, there's not one of them mentioned in the Bible. Old Testament or New, I defy anyone to show me a single mention of the Mass. Youse can believe anything youse want, I've got nothing against views sincerely held, but when I'm told that the wafer the priest holds up at Mass IS the Body of our Saviour, well then frankly I have to say what poppitipoo! Is it in the Good Book? I mean, if you stuck a knife in the wafer would it bleed?'

From his pocket he took out the penknife and with his pudgy fingers opened the major blade. The sun danced along its edge as he waved it in the air. The boy hardly dared breathe. Blade. Fist. They ruined hope and love.

'This knife here, if I stuck it in the Communion bread, do you mean to tell me it would bleed?'

The boy was petrified. Even Gore was watching now.

'Well, I'll tell youse what we'll do. Let's put it to the test.'

Snapping the lid of the harmonium shut he glanced at Tilly. Laying the handkerchief on the lid and with deft ceremonial fingers, like a priest placing the Corporal on the altar, she revealed the Host.

Bobby raised it up between finger and thumb.

'Now this here is a Host as you can plainly see and was used in Mass this very morning in the County Cavan and was given to me by my young friend here, who is like most of you, I'm sure, a practising Catholic.'

The boy's blood ran cold. Every eye in Bundoran was looking at him. He was dry-mouthed with terror. He could see from the dumbstruck faces that if they weren't all washed away in the blood of the Lord, they were quickly going to turn violent. Their beliefs were being held up to a terrible ridicule. Even a saint couldn't put up with that.

One man got to his feet, his trousers rolled up to his knees and a knotted hankie on his head. His face was a mask of amazed anger.

Bobby had the Host aloft in one hand, the knife in the other.

If it ever got back to Butlershill that it was he who had given him the Host he was as good as dead. He might as well walk out now into the ocean.

'If it bleeds I tell you, friends, this very hour, on my hands and knees, I'll walk to the nearest priest and beg to be converted.'

The penknife in his hand like a dagger, he put the Host on the harmonium lid and stabbed it three times. The dull clack of the knife on wood mocked the boy's fear and belief in the Eucharistic mystery. He could see the wafer on the knife point, the blade clean through it. There wasn't a single drop of blood. Not one. The Atlantic rolled in and out and above the gulls ripped and tattered at the air.

Though deep in his brain he had admitted the possibility that the wafer was nothing but wheat mixed with water and flattened between two irons, he felt utterly empty and let down, bitterly so when he saw the triumphant look on Bobby's face.

He began to cry. Tilly gave him back the handkerchief but he didn't meet her eyes. To come to the sea and not be happy. To have your faith broken. He wished he was home with his mother. Surely she could give him hope. He felt a hand stroking the back of his head. It was Gore.

'Don't cry. We'll build a castle.'

He didn't answer Gore because he could see the man with the rolled-up trousers and knotted hankie gathering a crowd around him.

Bobby, oblivious, was crowing to the beach.

'You see, when Christ died on the cross it wasn't fake. It wasn't a cross of fantasy, the nails that went in weren't pins. They were six inchers made of steel in a nearby Roman forge.'

Tilly shrieked. The mob was upon them, kicking over the organ and swiping with fists and handbags. Bobby reeled around, genuinely shocked.

'What, what have we done wrong? Ah come on, please now.'

'Away the hell outa this. You're not wanted here,' a woman shouted.

'What about religious liberty?' Tilly spat back.

'Get going, you witch. You only came to cause trouble.'

A man with a rolled-up newspaper hit Bobby across the face, knocking his spectacles on to his chest, where he instinctively caught them.

'Get goin', you Antichrist, or I'll be dug out of you.'

The boy and Gore fled up the beach, Tilly running after them, her shoes and hat in her hands. Bobby struggled in the rear with the harmonium. When he finally reached the van they all tumbled in and, with a shower of thumps and curses pelting them, at last bucked away from the kerb. Through the back doors which were swinging open, the boy could see the man with the knotted hankie on his head, running after them. He and Gore were sure he was going to manage to clamber aboard. He was derisively waving Bobby's captured bow tie at them.

'Ye feckers come back here again and it's dead ye'll be.'

At last the van gained speed and, with a great roar from the engine and exhaust, rattled out of Bundoran.

From the front came wild whoops and hysterical laughter and, rocking crazily along the twisted roads, they slowed down only when they crossed the Border into Fermanagh.

A belief destroyed hurt the same as a fist. The shame of Bobby Roberts with his saucepan face revealing the flat truth to him. What else was false and what was the point of bells and candles and holy water splashing on coffins as they were lowered into the grave? No blood, no magic. There was no man in the moon and probably no Santa Claus either. And all those years he had lain in bed, petrified by the bleeding crown of thorns and bared burning heart of Jesus hanging on the wall.

Gore's eyes were resting on him.

'The whole way there and just one ice cream. Never as much as stuck our toes in the water. No slab toffee or nothing. I'm going to start smoking cigarettes next week. Will we measure our mickeys?'

'I don't want to measure mickeys any more. So don't ask me. I don't want to do anything any more.'

'Because there was no blood? But even if there had been, we still wouldn't have got slab toffee. We'd have all been washed into the friggin' sea.'

He was even angrier when they sped through Enniskillen without stopping.

'That's crummy, that is. I'm starving.'

He tried to work out why he had taken the Host in the first place. What possessed him? Was it because of

Tilly? If only he hadn't done it, mystery would still be in his head.

When they turned off the main road and blundered down a country lane, to get a better look he and Gore pushed open the rear doors with their feet. Brambles and branches swept the sides of the van as they proceeded along a rutted path just wide enough for access. Swinging to a halt in front of a small whitewashed cottage, Bobby got out and went straight in the cottage door.

Almost immediately he came out again, carrying with the help of a young man a three-piece suite of furniture, which they loaded into the van. Then from a shack adjoining the cottage they carried a television set and a cardboard box of radios.

'Have youse time for a quick cup a tay?'

'No, no, honestly, we're in a shockin' hurry.'

For the remainder of the journey, he and Gore lay together on the sofa.

'I'm so hungry I could eat tin.'

'Me too.'

'What's your favourite food?'

'Rice pudding and jam.'

'Yeah and custard on it. And slab toffee.'

'And honey to my heart's content.'

The cottage from which they had smuggled the furniture was along the bank of a river. In the evening sun the water sparkled like a glassy snake broken across the fields. A man rowed a girl in a boat.

Somehow that was mysterious. And smuggling was mysterious. And so were Gore's hunting eyes. A thought floated into his brain. He had got the courage to steal the Host after touching Tilly's leg. He had always believed the Host was flesh. She was flesh. The burn he got from her was hotter than Communion. He was beginning to understand. But still wished it hadn't happened.

In Butlershill as he got out of the van Tilly smiled at him.

'Don't you tell anybody and we won't tell anybody.' The worst threats were always wrapped in smiles.

When he got home all hell and heaven flew at him. His mother, crying with relief, tried to fold him in her arms, whilst his father aimed whacks at his head.

'Where the hell have you been?'

'Darling, darling, we were so worried.'

'You were seen going off with that Gore Kemp.'

'Leave him, stop, can't you?'

'I tell you, me buck, you have it coming to you.'

Like a rat in a trap, he decided to scream louder than pain. He could feel his face go blue and green with panic, tears and howling. His brain was air and bubbles. He couldn't face it all so he let go and hit the floor in a dead faint.

His father was lifting him on to the bed and his mother was damping his face with the cloth that smelled of carbolic soap.

'It's all right, you're all right, take it easy, take it easy.'

'Say something, darling. Can you speak?'

'Course he can speak and no need to shout. He's not deaf. Yet.'

'I went with Gore to Bundoran. I only wanted to see the sea.'

His mother's tears fell on him as she hugged and kissed him. His father put his massive hand on his forehead.

'He's warm. But he'll live. All he needs is his dinner.'

His father smiled and stroked his hair back, calming him. He could feel the welts on his hand.

'I'm sorry, Daddy. I'm sorry, Mammy.'

When they both kissed him, he could see they were for a few seconds holding hands.

He had survived. Sometimes softness was hardness. Weakness was strength.

His mother brought him his dinner on a tray. And when she came to kiss him goodnight, sat holding him.

'I know a secret. But I won't tell a soul.'

'What?'

'It was you started the fire. Am I right? Tell the truth and shame the Devil.' She could corner him like no one else on earth.

'How did you know?'

'That night I found the box of matches in your pocket.'

She smiled a troubled smile of triumph. She knew everything.

'Arson is a terrible crime, you know. Of course you didn't really mean it, did you? Poisoners and arsonists can never be cured, God help us.'

'I'm not a criminal, Mammy.'

'Of course not, darling, of course not. What else did you do in Bundoran?'

What did she mean what else? He hadn't told her anything at all.

'Played on the sand and splashed in the water. And we had ice cream.'

Was Tilly Roberts an arsonist? She had set him alight for ever. And poisoned his belief.

'Mammy.'

'Yes, darling?'

'Supposing . . . you know the Host, the Communion Host? Well, supposing that was taken by somebody and they stuck a knife in it . . . and it didn't bleed . . . what would that mean?'

Her face was wide with fear as she looked hard at him.

'It would depend who was doing the stabbing, wouldn't it?'

'How do you mean?'

'Well, was it a Protestant person or a Catholic person stuck a knife in the Host, God bless us?'

'A Protestant person.'

'Well, that's your answer. Of course it wouldn't bleed for a Protestant. It only bleeds for Catholics. It's faith that makes the miracle. Now go to sleep like a good lad and I'll see you in the morning.'

All night he dreamt of Tilly soundly sleeping like a bell.

OJUS

AS OFTEN AS HE could, he escaped from the barracks to roam the drumlin fields or sit with the farmers in hedge or house until the rain had stopped.

There was water everywhere. In the sky, in the lakes, in the light; running off the hills, off the trees, off the roofs and cornered into barrels; in the lime-bottomed well, in the village pump, in the rain gauge at the rear of the Station, always in the air and constantly on tap in women's eyes and children's hearts.

'They're born with water in their veins instead of blood,' his father said. Bucketing rain they called 'A damp class of a day'.

In summer he watched George Conlon trying to machine the meadow land and being forced in the end to use a scythe. The swathes lay for weeks trying to dry in the skimpy winds between showers.

A constant net of drizzle hung from hill to hill, the people trapped as fish.

Their lives were moist, their words dry.

'That's a bad downpour.'

'I have me share of it.'

Words gurgled in their mouths like water going down a drain. It was a liquidy language, cranky, flat, sticky as strong tea.

'Why is Butlershill like a springin' cow?'

'Why?'

'Cos it's near Cavan.'

'I don't get it.'

'The bull did.'

In his innocence he had left himself wide open for a double punchline. Conlon tried to explain it to him.

'It's a bucolic joke with a sexual bent depending on geographical word-play. The cute hoors love someone like you. They've nothing better to do.'

They lived on dumpy hills rising out of water, along a political Border miles from Dublin or Belfast. Their cut-off lives ran long and narrow as a sheugh but their hearts were open to the boy and from morning until dark he helped them from the ploughtime of the year to harvest home.

'Give that lad a ponger of milk. He's earned it. Are you able for another hunk of bread? Course he is! What'll you have on it?'

'Jam, please.'

'Which one?'

'Rhubarb and ginger, please. It's the best I've ever tasted.'

'Ah-ha, he's the little smiler can charm the missus.'

On the good days when the sun got lost above them

he knew it was the greenest country in the world. The golden light magnified the green of grass and ivy, geraniums in window boxes, the glinty eyes of basking pikes. On golden days, bone of earth and rock screamed green to the hidden marrow.

'That's an ojus day.'

'You have your share of it.'

His window and the light were out of joint. The sun could only just sneak into his bedroom. It slithered over the sill, down the wall, across the lino, beaming for a few moments into the empty fireplace.

Good days, bad days, being out was freedom from the damp within. In the woods and lakes and hills was happiness. He couldn't bear the thought of being sent away.

The first he heard of it was from George Conlon. They were working in a turnip field, following a horse-drawn slipe, when Conlon stood up to light a fresh cigarette from the butt of the old.

'We'll miss you when you go.'

Puzzled, the boy stared at him. A mesh of drizzle gusted up from behind a hedge, falling sticky on his face like prickly sweat. He hated pulling and snedding turnips. A lumpy cold vegetable, his fingers were the same colour as them – freezing blue. Their tufts of turquoise leaves looked like fantastical wet ears and the sleeves of his cardigan were soaked with touching them. The gungy earth clodded his boots, and the water in the shallow drills slurped through his laces.

'I'm not going. Tea won't be ready for ages yet.'

Conlon gasped the smoke into his lungs. Adjusting his brown hat he looked at the boy.

'No. I mean when you go away to school.'

The part of the hat he held when putting it on and off was black from use.

'I am at school sure.'

He could see from Conlon's eyes he regretted having spoken.

'Maybe your mammy hasn't told you yet. She doesn't like the beatings that go on where you are. You're going to a boarding school instead. That's what she told me anyway.'

Lifting the rope reins from the slipe he flapped them over the horse's back. 'Up there.'

The mare rumped along the required few yards, wet earth falling from its huge hooves.

Panic could stab at you anytime, anywhere. Even in a turnip field. In an attempt to keep dry he had a slit potato sack, like a cowl, over his head and back. Throwing it off he bolted across the drills, through a sodden pasture, into the farmyard and out the drive on to the road. He had never known such fear grip his heart. He couldn't imagine his mother wanting to send him away. She needed him. How could there be miles between them, especially at night? It would be like death. And what would be the point of life without his father? He was frightened of him, he hated him but he loved him too.

He loved him in the mornings when he turned round from shaving, cut-throat in hand, to wink at the boy and laugh when he tried winking back. He loved him when his father held his hand tight, giving him his strength. He loved him when they swam in Kilifana lake, his father shouting, 'Isn't it grand to be alive?' He loved him when he told him stories of his own father, Black Jack, and his uncle Red Mick.

'I saw the pair of them drag a dead horse up on to a cart. With nothing but their bare hands.'

He loved to see him saunter through the village in his dark-blue uniform, high and handsome as a star. He loved him when he held his mother's hand and sang as best he could, 'In Pasadena where grass is green now . . .'

He wasn't going to go away to a boarding school. He would never leave Butlershill and all the people who fed him and let him sit at their open fires until night came down.

Running pell-mell, blind with fear, he came into the village. The tethered goat was crying on the green. He always stopped and spoke to it but now he cut straight past and up the hill to home.

Going by the forge the blacksmith shouted to him.

'How's she cuttin', gauson?'

He was in too much of a hurry and far too angry to reply.

He was so angry he didn't notice the car parked outside the Station. Tearing round to the married quarters and without taking his mucky boots off, he hurried straight into the kitchen.

'I'm not going to be sent away and don't try, so I'm not.'

The kitchen was empty. Where on earth was his mother? He was going to roar and shout and kick the furniture when he saw her. He wasn't going to be sent away. She sometimes rested in the afternoon. He ran down the hallway and crashed in through her bedroom door.

He could feel his dirty boots skittering to a halt and his face crumple in amazement.

She was sitting on the bed, her vest and blouse pulled up over her face so he couldn't see her face. Her naked breasts and belly were exposed and a man bent down towards her as if listening to something. The man couldn't hear him and his mother couldn't see him. Her arms crossed over her face held up her garments.

Her belly was white and round, her breasts bigger than he could remember. The man turned and looked at him. It was Dr Langan with a stethoscope hanging from his ears.

'Hello, young man.'

His eyes were riveted on his mother's belly. It was round, round as a moon. He was so shocked the world might have stopped turning.

His mother, lowering her arms, smiled, embarrassed.

'I thought you were helping George Conlon, darling.'

Something of the utmost importance was happening but his brain was in such a state he couldn't reason it out.

'Well, young man, you're not going to be on your own much longer. The baby is coming along very nicely indeed.'

That was it. A baby. His mother was going to have a baby. It was in there in her moony belly, waiting to come out and take his place whilst he was banished to a boarding school. The injustice of it was so startling he couldn't move, ask a question, shout for justice or run from the room and cry for mercy in a ditch.

'Go along, darling, there's some red lemonade in the meat-safe. Dr Langan will be going soon.'

Tears squeezed out his eyes and ran down the sides of his nose.

He walked out into the drizzle and stood dumbly staring at his feet. A curlew speared along the hill behind the barracks, its fifing notes drowning behind it in the rain.

Where was his father? He'd appeal to him. His mother wanted him out of the way so she could enjoy the baby unperturbed. If they tried to send him away he'd run into the demesne, climb the trees and live there like a bird.

He went into the barracks, anger swelling his heart. His father was in the day room with Guard Hegarty. They looked at him in huge amused surprise as he began to rant and rave and stamp the wooden floor.

'I'm not going to no boarding school. I don't want no baby. I'm not leaving here. You want to get rid of me. I'm not going. I'm the big and only bab. I'm not going to be sent to school in Monaghan. I want Mammy. I want Mammy.'

His rage suddenly draining from him he sunk to the floor, tired and breathless.

His father and Hegarty were laughing. He felt a fool. As soon as he felt his father's hand on his head he lashed out with foot and fist trying to hit him. Their guffawing laughter tortured him.

'Begad, Sergeant, he must have got out the wrong side of the bed this morning, hah?'

His father swung him up on to the table and, standing in close to him, imprisoning him, blocked him so he couldn't kick out.

'Now look here, will you calm yourself for Heaven's sake? You're going away for your own good. The school in Monaghan is far better than the one here. Where you won't get thrashed and the teachers won't come in half-shot or hungover. And the baby when it comes will be the best thing ever happened to you. Mark my words. A baby brother? A baby sister? Man alive you won't know yourself.'

His father's face was inches from him, his earnest eyes dancing, his lips now tight and serious, now smiling with conviction.

'Why didn't you or Mammy tell me?'

'We were going to, when we got round to it. Nothing we're going to do is going to be for anything but your own good. You know that, don't you? Hm?'

'I'm not going, I'm not going, I'm not going.'

Dr Langan tapping on the window, his father went out to talk to him.

Hegarty from deep in his trouser pocket handed him some coins.

'There's nothing like a bag of sweets to cure a fellah's heartache.'

He went out the main door, squeezing between his father and Langan who were sheltering from the rain.

They had planned the whole thing behind his back.

He'd be sent away and when he came back there'd be someone else in his place, taking his food, stealing his kisses, sleeping by his mother's side. How could his parents betray him so?

He went into the demesne and sat on his hunkers against a tree, his mind grim and desperate.

He hated the baby already. Because he was afraid of it. It would definitely limit his mother's love and his father would be all strutting pride. His father wanted lots of children. His mother had locked her door against him but since he had been forced to sleep on his own, he knew his father was going in to her and staying there for a good while before going back to his own bed. He sometimes lay awake listening to his mother's laugh. Laughter in the night burst out of mystery and was always followed by a deep secret silence.

The school he went to in the village he had to admit he didn't like. It had two teachers – a woman and a man. Being young he was in the woman's class but when she wanted children punished she sent them to the Principal's room. There in front of a wall-sized map of Ireland they were beaten without mercy. A cane was used – on hands, legs, back. Ears were twisted, hair pulled out in lumps. He had watched a friend being beaten until he sunk, crushed, to his knees. He had seen pools of urine on the seats, left there by frightened girls.

The boy was terrified. But why should a boarding school be any different? If he was beaten there he wouldn't have his mother to calm and soothe his wounds. They might as well send him away to jail.

Getting up he walked deeper into the wood. Round by the lake he met Lady Sarah Butler-Coote. She could tell straightaway he was unhappy.

'Oh, treasure, all alone? No chums? Do tell me what's the matter?'

Her old kind face and words turned him on like a tap and his fears came out in such a torrent of self-sorrow, a flock of ducks took fright and shot from the water, wheeling away above the trees.

'Oh my, oh my, oh my. I understand now. Hm. Boarding school? I do not approve of that at all. They sent me to one of those places too. The baby, though, that's golden news. It means you won't be alone in the world. Do you see? I wish I had a brother or sister. I wouldn't be all alone now. Rattling round the house like a pea in a biscuit tin. A baby? Oh yes, I approve of that. And so will you, my treasure, believe me you will.'

Her accent was rich and clear as music from a clarinet. He walked away, letting her words swirl round his head, testing them for sense, trying to defeat their purpose. She agreed with him about being sent away and if she was lonely why didn't she buy a husband? She didn't need a brother or sister at all. She loved animals, birds, fish, trees, children. None other came willingly near her. Her looks were legendary and deterred all comers. But surely her vast wealth could blind a desperate man?

When he arrived home, soaking wet, his mother scolded him for his sulking silence.

'You're a big boy now. You have to face up to things. I was a boarder, don't forget. With the nuns in Gortnor

Abbey. It'll cost money but we want you to have the best. And the day the baby is born, if all goes well, I'll send for you straightaway, kiss you and tell you I love you as much as ever before. Now that's a promise and you know I never break a promise, don't you?'

She was angry when he didn't respond.

'Do you know something? You're just like your father! The image of him in every way.'

Her words chilled him, tumbled his pride. He went to his room and sat on the bed for hours.

Events had hammered him into a corner and hard as he tried to escape over the following weeks, he couldn't. Everybody in the village and the surrounding farms knew about the baby and knew he was being sent away.

'I hear tell the stork's going to be landin' on the barracks chimney.'

'Boarding school? That's ojus altogether.'

Ojus was the most common adjective or adverb. It could be applied positively or negatively to any person, place or thing or stuck in front of any verb. It was a neutral word that could mean anything.

'We're going to miss you somethin' shockin'.'

He was going to miss them, that he knew. He couldn't think how he was going to manage to say goodbye.

His mother let him feel her stomach.

'It'll arrive in three or so months. If all goes well.'

'How do you mean, Mammy? It will go well, won't it?'

Without reply she went out and hung a line of clothes stretching the whole length of the garden.

He began to awaken early and, drawing the blinds, lie for hours looking out at the dark clinging to the trees, and the pigeons and pheasants striding about the field in the growing dawn.

One morning he saw Tully, the rich publican and shop owner, walking quickly past his window. Something must have happened. He was in such a hurry he wasn't even bothering to try and rouse the Guard who slept each night in the barracks dormitory.

The boy hopping out of bed had the hall door unbolted just as Tully knocked.

'You're a light sleeper, young fellah. Will you tell your daddy there's been a break-in at the lock-up shop out at Scotshouse Cross? Ojus amount of damage and destruction done. You'll not forget, will you?'

The lock-up shop was miles from the village and saved the people who lived in its vicinity having to journey for provisions. A shopboy worked in it during the day but at night it was empty.

Tully was the first man up in the morning and the last to go to bed. He thrived on work and worry. As long as he was moving he was making money. It was seven o'clock with a nippy breeze moving through swirls of cold mist. But Tully wore only his brown boots, trousers, braces and an open-necked shirt. He was a lonely bachelor. There was no one to keep him in bed. The boy wondered why he and Lady Sarah didn't get married. Two peas in a biscuit tin were better than one.

Later, he went down to his father and told him about the break-in.

'Well, bad cess to them whoever it was. And Tully. Put the kettle on.'

The boy could see he was secretly pleased. This was crime. Not a murder maybe, but a mystery to be cracked. Someone to be trapped by evidence that had to be hunted out. It was what his father loved. His dream of course was murder.

'One good murder is worth a thousand bicycles without tail lights. It's worth a hundred car crashes. A pub-full of after-hours drinkers doesn't compare. Murder is the only reason police exist.'

He watched his father shave, the cut-throat razor held delicately in his hand as a broken wing. He was humming, pleased with himself. The boy could smell the thick shaving lather from across the other side of the kitchen. It came squeezing out of its tube on to his father's hand like a green caterpillar.

'If it wasn't tinkers did the break-in, then I'm a Dutchman.'

'It might have been a travelling criminal, Daddy.' The boy knew the terms and enjoyed drawing his father out.

'As the Scotsman said, I have me doots. Tully said there was a lot of damage done, didn't he? That's the tinkers for you all right. Housebreaking with destruction – it's bred into them.'

'This can't be housebreaking, can it? A lock-up shop isn't a house, is it?'

'It's classified as such under the Larceny Act, 1916, Section 26.'

'How will you proceed with the investigation when you arrive at the scene of the crime?'

'Light the Primus and do me a boiled egg and don't be annoying me. Oh cripes.'

A seed of blood pushed out from a nick on his lip and spread like red ink over his soapy mouth.

'Why is the Primus stove made in Sweden, Daddy?'

'Do you want me to cut meself again? I don't know why! It's an impossible question. All I know about Sweden is two things. They're famous for hardy sailors. And they make Primus stoves. Nothing else.'

'If there are any footprints at the scene will you take a cast of them?'

'You've reminded me, good boy. Go round to the dormitory and get the bag of plaster of Paris from the top of the wardrobe. I'll be needing it for certain.'

His father was happier than he had ever remembered him. Whistling, relaxed, calm. There were no epileptic roars in the night or moods in the day. He took his daily pill, spooned Milk of Magnesia if his stomach was upset and, after long rides round his sub-district, gulped his glass of barley water.

'Keep the bowels regular and God will look after the rest.'

He rode away from the Station, the bag of plaster of Paris buckled to the carrier by its thin, fraying leather straps.

His mother calling from her bedroom sent him down to Reilly's for bread, butter and a box of matches. And the newspaper.

Reilly moved slowly behind the counter, letting the day seep gently into his bones. He was tall with handsome smiling looks and a quick temper which he used to poke conversation from all who went in to him.

'What are you looking so happy about?'

'I'm being sent away to school.'

'Pity about you. Wasn't I sent to the same school meself?'

'Were you? What was it like?'

'Rough in them days. Not any more from what I've heard.'

'Do they beat you?'

'Only if you shoot the teacher.'

The boy laughed.

'You'll have the time of your life. There'll be fellahs from all over the country, just like yourself. You won't want to know us when you come home on holidays. How is Mammy keeping?'

'Fine, thank you.'

He went home knowing his days were numbered. There was no escape. He would have to obey.

Smoke was rising from the Station chimney. Through the day-room window he could see Guard Hegarty down on one knee rattling at the fire with a poker.

In the kitchen he put the groceries on the dresser, spread the newspaper on the table and turned on the wireless. Jazz, all the way from New Orleans, blew round him like a hot wind. Standing at the table, listening, reading, he was content.

Thinking he heard his mother call he turned the

wireless down. The door opening she staggered in, bent double, clutching her stomach, her face deathly pale.

'Oh no, oh no, oh please, God, no.'

The boy saw dark water breaking down her legs, then blood.

'Don't be frightened, darling. Get the doctor quick.'

In the day room Hegarty phoned for the doctor and when he raced back to the kitchen his mother was lying in the armchair, her stomach heaving, pain, panic, regret in her eyes.

His blood was running cold, his brain half dead. Low, on the wireless, a clarinet cried.

'A towel, darling.'

He got a towel and a glass of water. Holding her hand he looked at her. She was crying like a child and in her face was enough sorrow for the whole world.

'Please don't die, Mammy.'

'Get one of the women.'

He ran to the nearest house and within seconds there was a flock of women running before him.

He hated himself. He had hated the baby and now this was happening. It was all his fault. Evil thoughts became evil deeds. Numb with heartache and guilt he knelt down on the roadside and prayed for his mother and for forgiveness. The occupants of a passing car looked out at him amazed.

Then on Guard Hegarty's three-speed bike he rode out to Scothouse Cross to tell his father.

He rode like a fury, his legs and lungs aching. He didn't care if he crashed. At least he wouldn't have to face his father and see the bad news rooting in his eyes.

He was selfish. Kicking up such a fuss about going away to school! What did it matter? If God would spare his mother he would willingly go the whole way there crawling on his hands and knees.

He shot by the Orange hall, the quarry, the Protestant church and a scatter of whitewashed houses with a barking dog at every gate. All the fields were pudding-basined hills flagged with ragwort. The potholed road was a rotten mouth, the hawthorn hedges on either side long thick lips red with lipstick. Reaching Tully's shop he flung the bike against the wall and went in.

He was aware of the destruction even as his father pierced him with his stare. Sugar crunched under foot. Big-bellied bags of flour were ripped open, their contents spewing. A box of butter was upended and walked on to a mash. The shop counter was littered with broken glass. A radio lay upside down, its back ripped off, the valves and workings kicked to pieces. Plaster of Paris dusted his father's trousers.

'Come quick. There's something wrong with Mammy.'

His father's face turned to stone. His body went rigid, his fists tight. His eyes glazed over and for a few moments closed.

'Sacred Heart.'

He went out, mounted his bicycle and methodically rode away.

To the boy it seemed as if his father had been half expecting the news. And knew how to steel himself to the moment. Perhaps it had happened before. Perhaps he was an only child because no other child had managed to make it from his mother's womb.

At the back of the shop, on muddy ground, was a large saucepan upside down as if covering something. On lifting it he saw a plaster of Paris cast. A footprint. The saucepan was to protect the plaster from rain or anyone accidentally treading on it.

The state of the shop was like his own state. Shattered. An alarm clock lying on a shelf began to clatter like a grasshopper, the hammer blurring between two bells. The glass was broken, the minute hand snapped. Abruptly it stopped. The world was a silent, chaotic place.

When he arrived home his mother was in bed, the doctor and his father with her. She was going to be all right. She was going to live. On the floor at the end of the bed was the foetus, wrapped in the *Irish Independent*. A death parcel. His own flesh and blood.

His father told him to dig a hole in the garden. He dug it beside a blackcurrant bush. He didn't want to dig it at the bottom of the garden because that's where they buried the contents of the Elsan lavatory. The ground there was sunken and spongy.

He saw his father coming carrying the parcel. His face was grim and grey as tallow. The corner of his lower lip was gripped in his teeth.

He took the shovel from the boy. Placing the parcel in the hole, he began to fill in the clay. Gardening was his favourite pastime. He spent as many hours at it as on police duties. With a shovel in his hand and clay before him he had the grace that comes from power and rhythm.

Patting down the top of the piled clay with the back of the shovel, he turned away and stared at the hill rising from the swampy field on the far side of the garden hedge.

His back seemed to tremble, his shoulders shake. It was the first time the boy had seen him cry.

Going to him he clung round his waist and his father, dropping the shovel, held him tight. They stood as one, crying bitter tears, his poor mother watching from her bedroom window.

'You're just like him,' she had said.

He knew his childhood was over. It would lie 'til Doomsday with his tiny dead brother or sister under the blackcurrant bush.

A week later they walked him to the railway station, where he would get the morning train to Monaghan. He would never have thought it possible but he was glad to be leaving. Since his mother's miscarriage the house was gloomy and dead.

Though it was before eight o'clock, doors opened and people rapped on windows.

'Goodbye, we'll be thinking of you.'

'Good luck now.'

'God be with you, you ojus boy.'

To his delight and his father's amazement, as they neared the station Tully hopped down from a lorry and, shaking the boy's hand, crinkled a pound note into it.

'We'll miss you, gauson, aye, man, surely.'

'Thank you, Mr Tully, thank you very much indeed.'

When they had walked on, his father muttered from the corner of his mouth – 'Wonders will never cease.'

'I always told you,' said his mother, 'Tully was a Christian man.'

Waiting for him on the platform was George Conlon. His parents protested when he handed the boy five pounds.

'Get away outa that, Sergeant, he earned every penny of it. And more.'

When they heard the train whistling in the distance, his mother began to weep. He put his arms around her neck. She was powdery, perfumed, fresh as apples. He clung to her, dragging her scent down into his lungs, feeling for the last time the heat that warmed his soul.

As in a dream he stepped on to the train and felt outside himself as he waved goodbye.

The engine thundered away with him and just before they went into the deep cutting, he saw Harry, Conlon's twisted brother, waving to him from the turnip field. He would have had to set off very early to make that distance from the house.

There were still stars in the sky and a crescent moon hanging like an incense boat.

The night before, when his mother was packing his suitcase, his father came into the room and gave him a plaster of Paris footprint.

'It's my own print. I did it as an experiment. You can show it to your class. I'm sure they'll find it interesting.'

It was an impression of the sole of his boot. The mark of the big seg on the heel was clear, as were the rows of studs. The plaster was the colour of salmon flesh. His father's foot was huge. Police feet. Clowns' feet.

Before he put his case on the rack, he took the footprint out and, leaning from the carriage window, as they crossed the Finn River, threw it in. He would never need reminding of his father's footprints.

Shane Connaughton is an acclaimed novelist, screen-writer and actor. His screenplay for *My Left Foot* was shortlisted for an Academy Award; the film won two acting Oscars. His short film *The Dollar Bottom* (1980) won an Academy Award for Best Short Film. *A Border Station*, his fiction debut, was a bestseller and was short-listed for the Guinness Peat Aviation Book Award in 1989. A later novel, *The Run of the Country*, was made into a film, for which he also adapted the screenplay. Shane's most recent novel, *Married Quarters,* a sequel to *A Border Station*, is now available. Originally from Cavan, Shane was brought up in a rural Garda station on the Fermanagh border. He is married with two grown-up children.

MARRIED QUARTERS
Shane Connaughton

An insignificant Irish border village at the tail-end of the 1950s. The Sergeant is nervous. His men are lined up for inspection in the day room of the Garda station. Chief Superintendent The Bully Barry is on the warpath and any slip-ups will reflect badly on the Sergeant. But what can he do with the men under his command – all of them forcibly transferred from other more important stations in more important towns? Each garda has his own story, his own problems. How can a man be expected to keep the peace with such a bunch of misfits and ne'er-do-wells?

Observing them with fascination, all but invisible in his own quiet corner, sits the Sergeant's son. On the cusp of manhood, he is drawn in by these rough and ready men, stuck in this place and time, when all he wants is a chance to leave and start his life anew. Life at home in the station's married quarters is both comfort and knife-edged, ruled over by his by-the-book father and his gentle, emotional mother.

Taking up where the acclaimed *A Border Station* left off, *Married Quarters* is a funny, brilliantly observed and deeply personal novel, and marks the return of Shane Connaughton, one of Ireland's most cherished writers.

Published by Doubleday